w.l
Pl

2 f

Occasional Poets

Occasional Poets

AN ANTHOLOGY

edited by
RICHARD ADAMS

VIKING

VIKING
Penguin Books Ltd, Harmondsworth, Middlesex, England
Viking Penguin Inc., 40 West 23rd Street, New York, New York 10010, U.S.A.
Penguin Books Australia Ltd, Ringwood, Victoria, Australia
Penguin Books Canada Ltd, 2801 John Street, Markham, Ontario, Canada L3R 1B4
Penguin Books (N.Z.) Ltd, 182–190 Wairau Road, Auckland 10, New Zealand

First published 1986

Edition and Introduction
Copyright © Richard Adams, 1986
The Publisher's Acknowledgements on pp. 179–82
constitute an extension to this copyright page

Filmset in Monophoto Bembo by
Northumberland Press Ltd, Gateshead,
Tyne and Wear
Printed in Great Britain by
Richard Clay (The Chaucer Press) Ltd,
Bungay, Suffolk

British Library Cataloguing in Publication Data
Occasional poets : an anthology.
  1. English poetry——20th century——
  Periodicals
  I. Adams, Richard, 1920–
  821'.914'08   PR1225

ISBN 0–670–80209–3

CONTENTS

INTRODUCTION

Some time ago, I happened to read four or five poems by a fellow-novelist, written, as he told me, 'at various times'. I said that I not only thought they were good, but that to me they seemed to form an integral part of his *œuvre*, complementing and to a certain extent enhancing what he had expressed in his prose works. Had he never considered publishing them? He replied that the idea was impractical. 'There are too few,' he said, 'and anyway, publishers aren't much interested in occasional poetry by writers who aren't regarded by the public as poets.'

'I appreciate that,' I replied. 'But would you *like* them to be published?'

'Oh, naturally. I think that in an ideal world anyone who'd written something – prose or verse – which he found he liked well enough to keep, would want it to be published. Sometimes, of course, occasional poems are very personal: but even when they are, that doesn't seem to make their writers reticent, does it? Look at Hardy – Yeats –'

Reflecting on this, and on the quality of my friend's poems and what they had succeeded in expressing, I came to realize that as regards content (as opposed to mode or technique), there can be no distinction in kind between prose and poetry: and soon afterwards, as though to endorse this thought, I came across the following passage in an essay by Evelyn Waugh on 'Literary Style in England and America':

'Properly understood, style is not a seductive decoration added to a functional structure; it is of the essence of a work of art. This is unconsciously recognized by popular usage. When anyone speaks of 'literary style', the probability is that he is thinking of prose. A poem is dimly recognized as existing in its *form*.' (My italics.) 'There are no poetic ideas; only poetic utterances and, as Wordsworth pointed out, the true antithesis is not between prose and poetry, but between prose and metre. Now that poets have largely abandoned metre,' (this, I suspect, was intentionally sardonic, for there is little or no evidence that Waugh himself had much natural predilection for modern poetry) 'the distinction has become so vague as to be hardly recognizable. Instead of two separate bodies of writing, we must see a series of innumerable gradations from the melodious and mystical to the scientific. Literature is the right use of language irrespective of the subject or reason of the utterance.'

If this is correct, it follows that everything a writer creates and does not destroy, whether prose or verse, should be regarded as part of his entire work.

Trollope has been injudiciously criticized on the grounds that he wrote in the early mornings and boasted that he could write at a steady rate of 250 words every quarter of an hour: to which C. P. Snow rightly retorted that when you came to consider it, it did not matter in what way a book was written; all that mattered was the quality of the book. Similarly – or so it began to seem to me – whether a writer was to be regarded as a poet, a playwright, a critic, an essayist or a novelist mattered less than the originality and veracity of what he or she said and of the quality of his style and technique. Ideally, nothing the writer himself had thought worth keeping ought to be disregarded.

It is safe to say that nearly everyone who writes seriously has at one time or another written poetry which he has chosen (consciously or subconsciously) not to cast aside. It seemed to follow that at least a fair proportion of those writers whose work in prose had already made them popular and widely read, would probably have, somewhere about them, verse or poems good enough to give their readers further pleasure and to interest them by being novel yet characteristic – a recognizable and well-known voice speaking, as it were, in a different cadence. (Here, by way of example, I refer the reader to the contributions from P. G. Wodehouse.) Such poems, I thought, could hardly fail to complement their writers' prose in an attractive and interesting way.

I determined to give it, as they say, a rumble. In order to be sure of obtaining enough to comprise a worthwhile anthology, I decided that it need not be a *sine qua non* that contributors should never have published any poetry whatever. The qualifications for inclusion would be first, that the contributor should already be known to the public as an author, playwright, etc., and secondly that he or she should not be regarded – or not regarded to any marked degree – as a poet, even though he might have published a slim volume or so.

The response was good and as things have turned out, only a small minority of the poems in this book have been published between covers before. None of the authors – and each has achieved at least something of a name, while a number are eminent – is thought of by the public as a poet. Yet I for one am in no doubt that the finished product – this book – demonstrates that the project has been worth undertaking.

It is only fair to add that my notion (though not the completed book) has been deprecated by a friend who *is* an acknowledged poet. 'Poetry is the business of poets,' said he. 'It takes years to unearth your own original gift and to develop and perfect your technique. People who write the odd poem now and then lack commitment and technique, and this alone makes their work not worth publishing.' I can only disagree. In this book there aren't, I readily concede, any undiscovered Eliots, Yeats or Audens. Yet writing poetry is a natural, spontaneous, human activity. In this respect it has something in common with cooking. Certainly it takes years to become a *cordon bleu* chef, and great chefs are unique and individual. Yet numerous amateur, lesser folk are not unhandy in the kitchen and can give genuine pleasure at the table, even though on a lower level. It is nice when they are people you know and like. The subjective, personal factor plays a large part; and this is true also of occasional poetry. Another analogy – that with music, from grand opera to folk-song – is too obvious to need developing. One recalls Wordsworth and his 'meanest flower'.

An ancient Greek – assuming there to be one on hand – would no doubt make the point that all poetic creation is the gift of Phoebus Apollo. (That is to say, some deep, psychological force, conveniently anthropomorphized as Phoebus Apollo, is feeding raw material in from somewhere beyond the conscious mind.) Certainly, to become a poet of stature the aspirant must specialize, must enter Apollo's service unreservedly and follow him year in, year out (Hardy gave up novels for poetry); and even then, perhaps, be rejected in the long run. Yet though capricious, the god is not without a certain all-embracing charity, and there have always been those whom he takes a fancy now and then to brush lightly with his wing; to impel to respond to emotion by writing poetry upon occasion – or merely for amusement. People find themselves acting, as it were, by his grace and favour. So general is the phenomenon that one could undoubtedly put together an anthology of poems by people who have never published anything. This could not, however, *ipso facto*, possess the same interest as an anthology by known writers putting on a fresh guise and appearing to their public in the unfamiliar rôle of poet.

W. H. Auden, in the long and delightful 'Letter to Lord Byron' which forms the *pièce de résistance* of *Letters from Iceland*, remarks

> Art, if it doesn't start there, always ends,
> Whether aesthetics like the thought or not,
> In an attempt to entertain our friends.

Here, I think, we come close to the true nature of occasional poetry (for which, incidentally, Auden had an outstanding gift). The idea for a poem originates in an impulse springing from a particular experience and the related emotion. The poet – he may not always know why – becomes sufficiently absorbed to take trouble over the poem; that is, he not only obeys his first impulse, but goes on to refine his work, drafting it, perhaps, several times and doing all he can to perfect it. Finished, it may even satisfy him – for about forty-eight hours, T. S. Eliot used to say. Having taken such trouble, he naturally wants others – or at least another – to read it – perhaps the lover who inspired it, perhaps a circle of friends; even, it may be, as many people as possible. He rarely has other than one of two purposes; either to amuse his readers with wit or humour, or else to move them emotionally. (It is significant, I think, that this anthology includes few narrative poems. This sustained verse form – probably because it is not spontaneous – seems to lie outside the field of the 'occasional poet'.)

The occasional poet's work usually comes very much from the heart – or from the shoulder. He feels it deeply and would like it to be published. Yet if he has no experience of professional writing, he is likely to lack a certain basic capacity for technique and self-discipline: in a word, 'polish'. Hence, while he will appeal to friends who know him and his circumstances, he is unlikely to do so on merits to a wider audience. This is what my poet friend was getting at in denigrating 'occasional poets'. The appeal of a serious, dedicated poet is due not only to his subject matter – to what he actually says – but also at least as much to his originality and skill in technique. Hopkins and Dylan Thomas, for example, were technical innovators of genius. That sort of thing is beyond the aim of the occasional poet. He just feels like writing a poem now and then; and sometimes it comes off well enough to give other people pleasure and earn him a degree of respect among his friends.

But when the occasional poet is a serious – even a professional – writer, then his poems are likely to be of considerable general interest, because they will be uttered in his distinctive voice, reveal his nature still further and throw new light upon the preoccupations and ideas which have already appealed to the public in his prose work. To take only two examples, the poems, included here, of Malcolm Bradbury and of William Golding are particularly interesting and moving.

In the long run, as George Orwell said, the only test of merit is survival. This is a splendid remark, for it holds out hope to everyone putting pen to paper. All manner of occasional poets and all manner of poems, including many trivia, have survived for centuries. In many cases, I suspect, the poets would be most pleasantly surprised and gratified. Who wrote 'Summer is y-comen in' or 'Jesu, sweetė sonė dear'? Would Robert Wever be surprised to learn that after more than four hundred years people still like 'In youth is pleasure'? And how about Charles Wolfe (dead at thirty), 'The Burial of Sir John Moore'; Francis Mahony, 'The Bells of Shandon'; or Eugene Field, 'Wynken, Blinken and Nod'? On a deeper note, one thinks of Dr Johnson's occasional poems. His true literary gift, as John Wain has rightly pointed out, was not for poetry; but no one who has read it is likely to forget his elegy for Robert Levet. A certain amount of poetry of at least acceptable quality is becoming to any man or woman of letters worth the name.

Finally, I would plead that this modest anthology has at least one indisputable merit. To make my point with full force, I refer the reader to Philip Larkin's essay 'The Pleasure Principle', in his book, *Required Writing* (Faber, 1983). A poem that is not enjoyed by readers, says Larkin, can hardly be said to exist in a practical sense at all. A poem must be emotional in nature and theatrical in operation. If it does not create emotion in others it is *ipso facto* a bad poem. Yet today (he goes on) we are continually confronted with poems which do not even try to move the reader and cannot be understood without reference beyond their own limits. 'Poetry has lost its old audience and gained a new one ... The poet ... can praise his own poetry in the press and explain it in the classroom, and the reader has been bullied into giving up the consumer's power to say "I don't like this, bring me something different." '

During the later middle ages many people, especially among the emergent prosperous middle class, found that in the press of business they had little time to spare for the observances of the Church. Yet they were not prepared to renounce or disregard them: that would have made them infidels. So what did they do? They endowed churches and chapels and paid professionals to pray and worship for them.

Something of a similar state of affairs obtains in the field of English letters today. The majority of literate people, I fear, have neither time nor inclination to read, e.g., *The Faerie Queene, Paradise Lost, Prometheus Unbound*, or even, I suspect, more than a little of the poetry of Yeats and Eliot. Yet they are not prepared openly to cast aside and deny acknowledgement to these great works. So lecturers and tutors are subsidized from public funds to teach them, and students are subsidized to study them.

Larkin, in a witty but depressing simile, compares the new-style, toiling and syllabus-bound reader of poetry to the ignorant partner of an unconsummated marriage, who has no idea of anything better. 'If,' he says, 'the medium is in fact to be rescued from among our duties and restored to our pleasures, . . . a revulsion . . . will have to start with poetry readers asking themselves . . . whether in fact they do enjoy what they read.'

Every poem in this book has been written for pleasure, without subsidy, without financial profit as a prime motive and with the sole objects of expressing emotion and moving or entertaining friends and others. Most are lucid and readily comprehensible. Whatever its limitations, there never was a less didactic anthology.

I thank all the contributors warmly, and hope that the book will redound in the eyes of the public to their greater credit and wholeness as writers.

RICHARD ADAMS

ACKNOWLEDGEMENT

The editor acknowledges with gratitude the invaluable help which he has received from his secretary, Mrs Elizabeth Aydon, not only in typing and preparing this book, but also in undertaking (with the clearest of heads and the best of memories for detail) the large amount of correspondence involved with contributors and others.

RICHARD ADAMS

Three Antipodean Sonnets

I. THE GREEN FLASH

'Come out on deck,' they said. 'Now the sun's setting
We might observe that rare phenomenon
Which those who've seen it say there's no forgetting.
Just for the briefest moment, here and gone,
The green flash glitters out of the horizon
As the sun vanishes; and that's a sight
To turn your head. Stand here, and keep your eyes on
The sinking disc. It might occur tonight.'

I saw the flash, Ammie. It was a green
And lucent blaze, haloed in dusky red,
Passionate, glowing; just an instant seen
And quenched. Yet on my solitary bed
I cannot sleep, remembering that keen,
Swift glance. That sea-green marvel's turned my head.

II. THE ALBATROSS

A trim, luxurious ship upon the ocean,
Controlled, secure in her magnificence,
Sure upon course, unfaltering in motion,
Your well-found heart's replete with confidence.
Zig-zag astern, I am your albatross,
Wing-tip to wave, hour after hour; perhaps
There'll be some bits. I veer, cross and re-cross,
Patient, alert and hungry for your scraps.

The wake foams white at night-fall. Gaze at me
Once more before you laugh and dine with friends.
I'll glide all night on my accustomed sea,
This solitude where love begins and ends.
Ammie upon the deck, you never heard
That famished love's tenacious as a bird?

III. RED HAIR

Do you remember how we went ashore?
The whorled canoe-prows painted blue and red:
The shell-and-bead gifts hanging at the door
Of the stilted hut, the lines of fishnets spread
To dry, and the drum carved like a crocodile?
The dark-skinned children followed you to stare
And point, till some, grown bolder in a while,
Reached up with shy, quick hands to touch your hair.

The others – they'll recall, in years to come
The sandy dancing-floor, the young girls bare
To the waist, and the chanting man who beat the drum.
I only see the children crowding there
About you, gazing, wondering, and some
Laughing with glee because they'd touched your hair.

Insomnia

They say that when one lies awake
It's toss-and-turningly;
But being sleepless for your sake,
I'm well content to be.

I see once more, with eyelids closed
In quiet, friendly gloom,
Those centimetres you imposed
Upon the Penguin Room.

I hear your whisper in the bow
Of the leaping zodiac,
'Darling, the bridge can see us now;
Go on, sit further back.'

It's nearly twenty hundred hours;
Dusky the tropic air.
The ice clinks in the whisky sours
And suddenly you're there.

I watch you in the long, clear glass
And silent, sip my wine.
Your eyes from those around you pass,
Look up, and meet with mine.

And now you're weeping as we part.
What were the words I groped for?
'It's not the ending, it's the start
Of all you ever hoped for.'

This silent April midnight blends
With those Pacific seas,
As smoothly as my thought extends
To your Antipodes.

I wait content till you come back,
And wish no least thing undone;
The happiest insomniac
From Halfmoon Bay to London.

Iris Murdoch

'Give me your hand.' 'The thorn beneath the rose
Has made me bleed.' 'That is what I intended.'
'To entertain?' 'No; I am she who sows
The seed.' 'And I the soil, gashed and unmended.'
'You see the naked lovers?' 'Their hot fears
Torment them, coupling in the bitter snow.'
'And yet observe –' 'I'm blinded by my tears!'
'Then you shall listen, but you shall not go.'

'Whose is that racking cough, that moan of pain?'
'An old man – he has travelled very far
To death – sits at a table, once again
Reading a letter.' 'Letter? An aching scar!
His teaspoon clatters on the polished grain.'
'I caught the echo from that frozen star.'

ALAN AYCKBOURN

Seven Fragments

(i)
Cat crouching cunningly concealed behind that curtain
You have carelessly
Left
Your
      Tail
         S
          h
             o
              w
          i
           n
         g

(ii)
Depending which courses they steer,
The thing comic poets most fear,
They'll either clash
With Ogden Nash
Or merely appear Edward Lear.

(iii)
He who rides tandem with a woman like you
Must resign himself to a monthly cycle.

(iv)
Passengers should please slew down
And be prepared to shew their tickets.
Please try not to obstruct the flew
Of thro' passengers,
Nor get into a stow.
But form a respectable, orderly quoo.

(v)
Here's an announcement. Quite soon, platform eight
Will shortly be leaving a few minutes late.
Would cynics on board please not draw the conclusion
The train is in motion. This simple illusion
Will soon be dispelled when at quarter to three,
Their friends on the platform reach Devon for tea.

(vi)
She who keeps a cat in bed
Can safely keep her maidenhead.
She's guarded by some safety claws
From puberty to menopaws.

(vii)
Since every day I spend with you
Seems like a minute,
Whilst every hour I spend alone
Like a year,
It could be argued
That you're shortening my life expectation.
Not that I mind dying young
So long as you make it worth my while.

BERYL BAINBRIDGE

Three Poems

[Ms Bainbridge wishes readers to know that these poems were written during her adolescence.]

(i)
Shall I pause, remembering that one?
How the beech leaves fade and whiten!
Do I dare to show compassion?

Shall I make my hands stretch out?
How still the little churchyard lies!
Do I dare to grow devout?

Now the beech leaves rot and fall.
How still the little churchyard lies!
Let compassion shut thine eyes.

(ii)
We walk in the rain, not caring.
Tenderly we care not, walking,
How the larger world is faring.

Hold my hand, my nicest boy.
Holding hands is making certain.
In my heart now love is singing,
Fetchingly I sing now, finding
All that life to me is bringing.
Squeeze me close, my nicest boy,
That way songs shall cease for joy.

(iii)
If my mother stops her crying
And my father stops his shouting
At my Auntie Nellie's singing,
Will I too forget my whingeing?
If my brother does his practice
On the piano every week,
Will my mother stop from sobbing,
Bend to kiss me on my cheek?
If my Grandad lends us money
And the bills are paid at last,
When the autumn leaves are dying
Will my mother stop from crying?

Vatican Trouble

The team from the Sacred Heart
Was thin and whitish pale.
The lads from the grammar school
Were ruddy, red and hale.
Or so it seemed to standers-by
Who waited for the start.

'What they lack in brawn,' we said,
'They make up in the heart.'
The rain was awful heavy
And the ball was slow to rise.
The lads from the grammar school
Tried hard to stem the tide;

But on they came relentlessly,
And fought and hacked and – goal!
The grammar lads were mortified;
What did they know of soul?
But in the end the grammar lads
Fought back and won all right.
By gum, we thought, there'll be all hell
In the Vatican tonight!

RACHEL BILLINGTON

Catherine

[Note: Catherine Pakenham was killed in a car accident.]

The indecisive rows of dresses hung in your wardrobe
When I went to clear your flat:
The shoes below, the handbags in neat piles above;
In the kitchen, a special line in painted Chinese bowls.
The books along your shelf were partly
What you hoped to be and partly
What you were.
I cried, of course. It was damp there;
You thought so yourself, and outside
It started to rain.
I brushed into the dustbin your bottles
Of creams and oils and slimming pills.
I put aside to keep the bottle of wine
You bought to celebrate; and a new plant
Called 'Sweetheart', and other more acceptable mementoes.
The things that had touched your body were unbearable.
Those we gave away.
They didn't mean much to you, I know,
You hadn't started yet to make a final
Choice. There were more defeats than successes.
When the removal men, jolly, with square crates,
Came tapping at your garden window,
I wanted to say, I wanted to say
Be careful; be sad; cry with me.
These things you carry away belong
To my sister, my sister Catherine.

Peace

A rose leaf, pink threaded with green,
Bounces off the window.
The wind, elbowing in off the sea,
Catches it, plays with it, and then flies
Suddenly to the sky,
Where the clouds, clustering in figures of eight,
Pass shadowy above the grass.
This is an island. The horses
Who live here – below the clouds,
Above the sea – are furthest from where
I sit at my window, looking out
And wondering if peace is not here,
Where it is
Always buzzing in my head.

RONALD BLYTHE

Charles Edward

Briefly, in the Hebrides, I rose and set,
A promising six-months' sun.
The Minches grated on their strands,
The clans danced and roared.
Anything for an unquiet life.
Brave and pale, young and fooled,
I leapt from the *Doutelle*
And the Scotch islands caught me in their arms.

'I have come home with my little crew,' I said,
'To collect the three crowns for my father.'
And they believed me. Although
'Go home,' they said; but only at first,
So as to sound wise before the event.

In no time we were skirling over the Sleat
To Glenfinnan, unfurling flags, all eyes south.
It was August and the harvest stood beseeching.
At night, shivering in stone chambers,
I dreamt of restored fortunes

And the warmth of Miss Walkenshaw.
Outside, my musky ranks, swelling by the hour,
Coloured the ground for miles.
Then, Edinburgh and the first crown.

We swarmed the Border at Kelso and were so happy
At Penrith, Shap, Kendal, Lancaster, Preston, Manchester,
That we scarcely noticed the French had not landed
And the English were sitting on the fence.
It was Advent when we engulfed Derby, and cold.
The talk was suddenly of skin-saving and turning-points.
I cried, 'London!' and was princely.
They were dutifully admiring, but all eyes north.

So, it was singing the retreat back
To that unspeakable moor,
And my highlanders butchered three deep,
Their blood runnelling through the Easter grasses.
And then the slipping back to Skye,
Where they were very good to me, considering.
I am old now, and a famous drunk, resident in Italy.
I blame the Scotch for seducing me
With their strong spirits.

Sligo, September 17th, 1948

(*The re-burial of William Butler Yeats*)

To honour him, a narrow, dipping ship,
A pall of hissing spray.
To follow him, white, wind-torn birds,
Tumultuous in his wake.
And then the late summer landfall,
The discrete boarding party, the lively,
Mourning pennants as his corvette
Noses the mist for the first solicitudes;
The welcoming, and the sounds of his own words,
For whose sake they have returned him.

MALCOLM BRADBURY

An Uninvited Guest

Behind the larder all is not quite well.
  The mice have made an entry, and a track
Leads, through the fresh-gnawed and unlikely hole,
  To some sparse nest; and even further back,

The path they came by through our solid wall,
  The hidden entry which we cannot find,
The frontier breached and no doubt open still,
  Creates a strange disquiet in the mind.

This house we live in is our very first.
  Securely battlemented by our love,
We thought our walls safe and our windows fast.
  Now in the wainscot we hear something move.

And then, tonight, we caught it in a trap,
  The mouse that had encroached into our rest,
Had spoiled our food, had dared to try and rip
  The paper linings to pad out its nest.

We set the trap to win our ease again
  Back from this small intruder in our peace:
And now, poor bugger, there it is in pain;
  And, torch in hand, we watch its struggles cease.

No, there it moved again, caught in the light,
    Its little eyes fixed on this tiny glare.
It tugs and writhes, grey thing. Its small paws meet,
    Grope, scrabble, grip piously in the air.

It must be killed. But who can kill the thing?
    A tear stands in my wife's betrayed, soft eye.
And I can't give the crude broom-handle bang.
    We go away and wait for it to die.

Inside our kitchen something is amiss.
    And when we go to bed tonight the mouse
Will not quite be forgotten when we kiss:
    Nor yet that there's a way into the house.

Evening Class

For twelve wet evenings, in the winter rain,
I've come in duty to this distant town,
Booked in at my hotel, cold off the train,
And, after dinner, made the long walk down

Past Dolcis, Woolworth's, shops with gramophones
And ice-white fridges shining in the dark,
And past the fish-dock, with its greasy stones,
The pubs, the tram-shed and the unlit park.

The town's a haven. I look at the boats.
The sea-wind comes in chilly as I hump
My briefcase, bulging with a wad of notes
On Auden's 'thirties writing on the slump.

I envy other travellers who sell
Their wares by daylight, and who now retire
Into the bar for residents, and tell
Commercial stories round the fake log fire.

The library is where I teach my class.
A wooden building, rebuilt where the war
Had pulped the books back into thick twitch-grass.
I get my key out and unlock the door.

For twelve dank evenings, sitting on these damned
Hard chairs, we've sat around, read poems, thought.
The winds, blowing in off the sea, have slammed
Our doors, brought many trawlers home to port.

A tiny light, switched on two hours a week
In this small library, has been our work.
Then we shut down – still lost from what we seek –
And leave the building to its usual dark.

The Pilgrim Fathers in Bloomington, Indiana

I once had a student, a dull, lumbering youth,
Who had a strange way of access to the truth.
He wrote in a theme, gross with illiteracies
(He was clearly more at home raising hogs or citruses):

THE PILGRIM FATHERS CAME TO AMERICA FOR FREEDOM OF
    RELIGIOUS PERSECUTION.

He had all the vain assurance of the prematurely old.
His personality was so well-rounded that it rolled.
He was skilled at How to Win People and Influence Friends,
Yet something in grammar allowed him to make amends:

DANTË HAD ONE FOOT IN THE MIDDLE AGES, WHILE WITH THE
    OTHER HE BECAME THE FATHER OF THE RENASCENCE.

How strangely comes wisdom, through a slip of the pen!
The universe speaks through the mouths of babes and freshmen.
He was apt by mistake; no one could find him a source
Of knowledge (and he failed, as you'd guess, in my course):

AND WHAT I HAVE SAID ABOVE IS A TRUE STATEMENT, AND CAN
    BE TAKEN FOR GRANITE.

Wanting Names for Things

I fetch a spade, and then I stop, deterred.
A little past would help me quite a lot
In learning how to tend these garden beds.
I am a new and untaught gardener,
A man out of the suburbs, who does not
Know which are flowers here, and which are weeds,
And what, beneath this brown and heated soil
Stirs and unfurls and germinates to life.

The flowers take the wind and nod their heads,
Varied and carefully charted. Here some seeds
Begin to yield their fruit. I ask my wife
Their names. But, Cuthbert pardon her,
She doesn't know either. We set to and toil,
Digging the garden over, hoping for the best.
Behind us, in the hedge, there is a nest
And in the nest there sits a nameless bird.

JOHN BRAINE

Your Word is Moorland

Your word is moorland: wild horses from the night,
Suddenly apocalyptic – what riders and what bright
Destination? The horses, movement; the moorland, stillness:
Dynamic and static: united, a symbol of love.

Your word is music: blind voice of radio,
The music that covers the heart like snow
And the words always, always unforgotten:
Votre âme est un paysage choisi.

Your word is rain: remembering how
We felt eternity's tension, then becoming now
And not tomorrow, the moments piling up
Unbearably in the sound of rain.

Your word is time: each tick of the clock
Is plain comment: nothing can chill the shock
Of time the lonely time because of you
And the days that gather like thunder.

Slacken the Pace of Prison

Slacken the pace of prison,
Unbolt the house of iron.
Release the hurting hand,
Break the green promise.

Morning in the black mad street:
O give him strength
To fight the windowclutching face,
To knife the tiger.

And in the end
His hot face to bury in the wind –

And in the end
His soul a cloud in the end to rain.

NEVILLE BRAYBROOKE

The Wise Men

Sometimes I like to think of the three Wise Men as Langland, Blake and
    Milton:
Langland setting out on a May morning with a gift of poems;
Blake on a tiger with a bow of burning gold;
And blind Milton led by an inner star.

The shepherds arrived first with their songs:
The poets were latecomers.

At Bethlehem we must imagine the scene for ourselves.
Was it a cave or a stable?
There is no way of knowing for certain.
The ox and the ass were the inspired interpretation of poets and others.
George Herbert added a horse and Christina Rossetti a camel.

One day the cave will become like a second Ark.
No longer will the lion roar in the depths of the jungle:
Quiet as a shadow he will slide in and lie down with the lambs
    and the mice in the rustling straw.

Sheep

Watching the sheep on this windswept down high above the sea
My thoughts have turned to the second Mrs Thomas Hardy
And how her husband instructed her to observe their many expressions –
Some cunning, some wilful, some frowning,
Some with the light of insurrection in their eyes,
Others docile and trusting.

Arriving before a ditch lined with stones they pause.
Who shall leap first?
Shall the first be last?

Now I think of another hillside where long ago on a winter's night
A host of angels encountered shepherds whom they greeted
With tidings of goodwill and peace to all mankind.
O shame on the new biblical translators
Who have directed the message to only those who are God's friends!
Among the flocks at Bethlehem were there no black sheep?

An Old Actor

I see him in the mind's eye as he was –
An actor of the old school purposely walking to the stage door by back
    streets.
A book of treasured press-cuttings confirms the past:
The Master Builder in Todmorden, *Oedipus* at Torquay – even a *Macbeth*
    when he was sixty.
He never played in London or New York.

On tour at each new town he would study the local map
So as to find a way to the theatre by the least conspicuous route.
When I asked him why
He paused – then answered slowly:
'Because, my friend, it takes away the mystery if the audience see you
    first.'

Joseph Speaks

I am tired of being thought of as an old man
Leaning upon a staff.
My beard is not grey.
Many miles did I pace the stable floor on the night of the birth –
And many more did I walk beside the ass bearing the Mother and Child
On our flight into Egypt.

Yet when poets and painters came to tell my story they altered the facts.
The painters gave my shoulders a stoop
And the poets shortened my stride to a shuffle.

They were mistaken:
They confused age with authority.

My passions were those of any young Jew of my tribe,
My senses as keen.
From my bench I watched the shadow of my espoused grow fuller.
Had I been deceived – and by whom?
Other women when found out had been stoned to death by the people.
But at night in dreams I heard voices promising to make perfect the
      impossible.
Sometimes the villagers spoke of two-headed goats
And of calves deformed at birth.
I said nothing.
I thought of the mysterious conception in my own house.
Was I mistaken when I heard the beating of wings?
(There were nests in the trees nearby.)
Words formed in my mind and became a consolation: 'Fear not, Joseph.'
Where did they spring from?
For beware – Pride in the heart can nourish the imagination.
So I said to my soul: 'Be patient, be still.'

The wings and the voices persisted.
My confidence grew in the Word.

The House of David would have a new Lord.

RAYMOND BRIGGS

Jean, 1975

It is eleven weeks
Since I visited my wife's grave.
It is not far away,
Just up the lane,
Five minutes' walk.
She has been dead
For two years and seven months.
The grass is long and rank,
When I cut it
The ants are swarming.
Nettles topple over the grave.
There are no flowers,
Just two empty pots
Full of dirty water.
Neither of them have I seen before.
Someone has been there.
One contains skeletons of roses;
The other pot is empty.
Someone has left a jar of Nescafé
Against the stone
And bird lime runs down its face
To where the lettering says
IN LOVING MEMORY.

BRIGID BROPHY

Nocturne

In the house, the mouse.
In the slum, the louse.
Pet mouse in his dainty box.
In his stall, the ox.

Pet mouse is kissed and put to bed
With sought-out delicacies fed,
Ignorant of the mice who snout
Through the wainscot and dash out
At an hour when human heads
Print soft pillows in snug beds,
While, though wintry night strikes raw,
The ox blows warmly in the straw.

When the master marries a wife,
A parsimonious housewife who tidies up,
The mice run away and end their life.
She leaves not a crumb for a mouse to sup.

In famine year of little yield
The ox roars hunger to the field.
He will be slaughtered to provide
Marketable flesh and hide.

In time of recession mouths are set:
'Frankly, we can't afford a pet.'

But when standards of living decline
Lice celebrate on blood-red wine.

Snow, 1980

Here and mad, mad and now.
The walls of my mind oscillate.

The pain you dealt me in a Nordic capital
Looks distant but snow-sharp, a picture
Of people vividly skating in
The seventeenth century.

Snow fell on us in Uzbekistan.
You gave me a snowman in a poem.
Final snow drifted from
The Stockholm sky. You volunteered
Allegiance to me as the Winter Queen
And you betrayed me icily.

Concourse

A pigeon on his stumps. An old woman on
The bottle. An empire
On its uppers.
                         'Excuse me. The tour
Leader is not at the assembly point. Is this
The Roman, the Holy Roman, the British or
The Austro-Hungarian Empire?'
'The inquiry office is shut.'

This station is named after
A queen named after a fact of
Victory.
They have forgotten the timetable.
                                    No less

They have forgotten
History.

A black man in uniform inflicts
Petty vengeance on everyone entering
Platform thirteen, but cannot remember
What historical acts it is vengeance for.

They try to expel the pigeons by
Threatening to fine you if you feed them crumbs.
Anyway the café is shut.
They try to expel derelicts by
Reducing the number of the benches and
Putting no chairs in the bars, which are shut
Anyway; and, should those fail, winding up
Pairs of policemen and heading them
In the direction of the derelict.

They have forgotten the names
They promised to remember for ever in
A list on the wall in ineffaceable,
Ugly lettering.
                        This is where
Troop trains left and returned as
Hospital trains
At a time when
The railways were more versatile.

The advance of the policemen, not even looking at
But conscious, in every chummy, dégagé muscle, of nothing except
One another, is a sexual act.

'Is this the Athenian or
The Corinthian League?'
                        A football follower
Vomits into the cracks in the concourse.

Flaming importunately beneath the nose
Of the woman I am with, a lighter pretends
Not to have realized that a woman so beautiful
Must have been often propositioned before.

A blind man's fingers read
The ugly, dead names on the wall.

They have mislaid the calendar. Look,
They have put up the Christmas tree
On midsummer's day.
                              The blind man's
Literate fingers are pierced
By a swag of artificial poppies,
The pigeons' feet by pine needles
And dolours.
                    Not before time, inside
An electronic oblong, effaceable
Lamé lettering records
A signal failure.

J. M. COETZEE

Dusk Seeps up the Entrail . . .

dusk seeps up the entrail of the seaborn nude
the vegetable sleeps in its circle
the bedroom drowses
the casino is swathed in tidal melancholia
the nude awaits the hero

mounting the entrail of the seaborn nude
toward the sleeping vegetable
toward the poisoned goose with its melancholy aftertaste
comes the naked philatelist of fiction

the philatelist climbs the entrail of the poisoned nude
who rules over the luck-swathed fiction
of castaway matriarch
punctual chimera
spider of solitude
the philatelist climbs the entrail of the nude
toward a bedroom where a sword drowses

the drowsy sword in the spare bedroom
of the casino in the tidal nude
awaits the philatelist of melancholia
through the symmetrical aftertaste of goose
the castaway philatelist gropes
he circles the poisoned casino
and enters the bedroom of the nude of solitude
where the sword of fiction drowses
the seaborn philatelist brandishes the sword of fiction

the nude feels the punctual sword in her entrail
is it the poisoned chimera she wonders
stirring in her entrail?
is it the symmetrical matriarch
the spare philatelist
the tidal goose from the castaway bedroom?
is it the bedpost of fiction
the aftertaste of solitude
the vegetable of melancholia?
is it the vegetable of melancholia mounting the entrail of the seaborn
    nude?
(what stirs in her entrail
is the punctual instrument of the drowsy philatelist)

in a drowsy circle near the punctual casino
in the tidal entrail of the lucky nude
waits the chimera of solitude
swathed in spare fiction
with castaway sword he beheads the chimera
the punctual philatelist vanquishes the chimera of solitude
and enters the symmetrical casino of fiction

the matriarch of melancholy sleeps in the tidal casino
the poisoned philatelist gropes through its symmetries
his search is perplexed
where is the seaborn matriarch?
without the seaborn matriarch where is the lucky fiction?

in the final symmetry of the casino of solitude
the poisoned vegetable mounts the sleeping matriarch

the philatelist arrives at the seaborn bedroom of the casino in the nude
as the spider mounts the symmetrical matriarch
the spare philatelist is filled with the melancholia of melancholia
upon the symmetrical matriarch he turns his castaway sword
and the tidal casino in the drowsing nude is filled with the fiction of
    solitude
the spare philatelist transfixes the punctual matriarch

the philatelist	the bedroom	the spider
the casino	MOONBURST	the goose
the matriarch	the sword	the fiction

past the sleeping vegetable and the poisoned goose
with its melancholy aftertaste
the castaway philatelist descends the entrail of the sleeping nude
but the nude of solitude is dreaming new dreams
the downfall of calligraphy she dreams
the documents of panic
the iron in the milk
the axes of sleep
the perfumes of the dead
the geography of caution
the crocodile of blood
the counterfeit footfall
the terrible tailor
the shadowy root
the feminine kingdom

QUENTIN CRISP

Now I am Dead

Now I am dead;
                    the cold, square house is shut
Where once I used to live and wonder why,
And every dark, uncurtained eye,
Though bleak before, is now a shade more bleak.

Upon the blue-green lawns the starlings strut
Where once I stood and hoped that I might die;
They strut and lance with sudden beak
The blue-green blades that no one comes to cut.

And on the pathways, tended now no more,
The raindrops, gathered on the underside
Of leafless boughs, drip as they dripped before,
And here I walk and wonder why I died.

ROALD DAHL

Song

(from *James and the Giant Peach*)

We may see a Creature with forty-nine heads
Who lives in the desolate snow,
And whenever he catches a cold (which he dreads)
He has forty-nine noses to blow.

We may see the venomous Pink-Spotted Scrunch
Who can chew up a man with one bite.
It likes to eat five of them roasted for lunch
And eighteen for its supper at night.

We may see a Dragon, and nobody knows
That we won't see a Unicorn there.
We may see a terrible Monster with toes
Growing out of the tufts of his hair.

We may see the sweet little Biddy-Bright Hen,
So playful, so kind and well-bred;
And such beautiful eggs! You just boil them and then
They explode and they blow off your head.

A Gnu and a Gnoceros surely you'll see
And that gnormous and gnorrible Gnat,
Whose sting when it stings you goes in at the knee
And comes out through the top of your hat.

We may even get lost and be frozen by frost.
We may die in an earthquake or tremor.
Or nastier still, we may even be tossed
On the horns of a furious Dilemma.

But who cares! Let us go from this horrible hill!
Let us roll! Let us bowl! Let us plunge!
Let's go rolling and bowling and spinning until
We're away from old Spiker and Sponge!

The Oompa-Loompas' Song

(from *Charlie and the Chocolate Factory*)

The most important thing we've learned,
So far as children are concerned,
Is never, NEVER, NEVER let
Them near your television set –
Or better still, just don't install
The idiotic thing at all.
In almost every house we've been,
We've watched them gaping at the screen.
They loll and slop and lounge about,
And stare until their eyes pop out.
(Last week in someone's place we saw
A dozen eyeballs on the floor.)
They sit and stare and stare and sit
Until they're hypnotized by it,
Until they're absolutely drunk
With all that shocking ghastly junk.
Oh yes, we know it keeps them still,
They don't climb out the window sill,
They never fight or kick or punch,
They leave you free to cook the lunch
And wash the dishes in the sink –
But did you *ever* stop to think,

To wonder just exactly what
This does to your beloved tot?
IT ROTS THE SENSES IN THE HEAD!
IT KILLS IMAGINATION DEAD!
IT CLOGS AND CLUTTERS UP THE MIND!
IT MAKES A CHILD SO DULL AND BLIND
HE CAN NO LONGER UNDERSTAND
A FANTASY, A FAIRYLAND!
HIS BRAIN BECOMES AS SOFT AS CHEESE!
HIS POWERS OF THINKING RUST AND FREEZE!
HE *CANNOT* THINK – HE ONLY *SEES*!
'All right!' you'll cry. 'All right!' you'll say,
'But *if* we take the set away,
What shall we do to entertain
Our darling children? Please explain?'
We'll answer this by asking you,
'What *used* the darling ones to do?
How *used* they keep themselves contented
Before this monster was invented?
Have you forgotten? Don't you know?
We'll say it very loud and slow:
THEY ... USED ... TO ... READ! They'd READ and READ,
AND READ and READ, and then proceed
To READ some more. Great Scott! Gadzooks!
One half their lives was reading books!
The nursery shelves held books galore!
Books cluttered up the nursery floor!
And in the bedroom, by the bed,
More books were waiting to be read!
Such wondrous, fine, fantastic tales
Of dragons, gypsies, queens, and whales
And treasure isles, and distant shores
Where smugglers rowed with muffled oars,
And pirates wearing purple pants,
And sailing ships and elephants,
And cannibals crouching 'round the pot,
Stirring away at something hot.
(It smells so good, what can it be?

Good gracious, it's Penelope.)
The younger ones had Beatrix Potter
With Mr Tod, the dirty rotter,
And Squirrel Nutkin, Pigling Bland,
And Mrs Tiggy-Winkle and –
Just How The Camel Got His Hump,
And How The Monkey Lost His Rump,
And Mr Toad, and bless my soul,
There's Mr Rat and Mr Mole –
Oh, books, what books they used to know,
Those children living long ago!
So please, oh *please*, we beg, we pray,
Go throw your TV set away,
And in its place you can install
A lovely bookshelf on the wall.
Then fill the shelves with lots of books,
Ignoring all the dirty looks,
The screams and yells, the bites and kicks,
And children hitting you with sticks –
Fear not, because we promise you
That, in about a week or two
Of having nothing else to do,
They'll now begin to feel the need
Of having something good to read.
And once they start – oh boy, oh boy!
You watch the slowly growing joy
That fills their hearts. They'll grow so keen
They'll wonder what they'd ever seen
In that ridiculous machine,
That nauseating, foul, unclean,
Repulsive, television screen!
And later, each and every kid
Will love you more for what you did.
P.S. Regarding Mike Teavee,
We very much regret that we
Shall simply have to wait and see
If we can get him back his height.
But if we can't – it serves him right.

SALLY EMERSON

The New Baby

I wonder if she knows
What she's in for.
Sometimes when I look at that
Knowing yet innocent face,
I see some ancient guru
Who has been here since
The world began
And yet has only just
Arrived.

Ten Weeks

Belonging to the early morning,
That distant period
When the dew lies on the ground
And a young world rules,
After the coming of the dark
And before the glare of the day,
You are still covered in dew
As you lie sleeping.

Back to Work

The world enters my body,
Runs its vast red buses
Through my stomach,
Swerves into my heart
Causing havoc.
Inside, telephones ring,
Typewriters ram their
Sharp metal keys into my mind.
There is dust on the windows, on the
Desks, on the piling paperwork.
Even the sunshine here is
Made of grey
And nothing is as it should be.

Meanwhile, my darling girl
Sleeps and smiles and laughs, her face
So full of curiosity and magic
That I know the world was
Made in her honour.
She looks around her and as she looks
She renews all she sees.
The leaves rustle excitedly,
The curtains dance by the window,
The shadow moves beside her as
She turns and she turns and she turns,
Ocean eyes,
Taking it all in.

JOHN FOWLES

Tourists at the Erechtheion

Mounting the famous marble hill,
The people come, the people stand
And stare; and then consult their guides,
But later stare again, since guides
Have never helped one here.

They see the sisters in the sun,
They try to tease their meanings out.
The too hermetic smiles upset:
What they know we do not know
Must be the joke they smirk about.

The endless tourists photograph,
Record each smile, then turn away
With trite awed faces, solemn looks:
Too humourless, too pale, too small
To grasp the sisters' point at all.

Straggling back to their plush hotels,
The same old blind Boeotian herd –
Some Paul should stop them, shout the truth.
No god can have a serious face:
It is the Smile that is the Word.

Julia's Child

You sit in a wind and cities fall.
I knew a poem by someone once.
Your tendrils in a disarray undo
my view. The highrise towers. You
mock my shears. Analyses of
market costs tend to become
the naked aspects of your thighs.
I ask for files to make you bend.

When you look grave, and I dictate
lies to your cool young mouth.
Green is the orchard, green
the shadows by the stream. I
dip hot fingers in your veins.
You are too fond of fabrics
stained with summer flowers.
Gravel and box, the contract said.

You cling and wind. You breathe,
you blow, you waft, you shift
the papers in my hands. You smell
of beaches. Tar and flume. Through
suit and collar and chartered tie
your zephyrs lick my untapped skin.
I am that night chair in your room
You throw your bra and briefs upon.

I am the soap that soaps your skin,
the naked sheets you lie between.
I am the secret sleepless hands
that stir on certain moonlit nights
and wake their breasts, then smooth
the nylon stomach down. You
belly-turn and bite the pillow
as you moan. I am the moonlight

on your back, I am the moan. I
am the goatman on your back,
I am the night. I am the sins
your young men lack. You kneel,
you give me well-trained lips to sign.
You sit astride, and I dictate.
I part your legs, and then you type.
You give me carbons when I want.

And none of these. We sit apart
and cities fall. Meanwhile I
rush appointments, miss good deals.
You are the odalisque of youth,
I am the eunuch of my past.
Nobody now believes my truth.
I am a brilliant company man
and crucified upon the mast.

Madness, visions, foul my desk.
I dream disorder all the day.
Each open door is your undress,
is your undress and lock the door,
is lock the door and standing there,
is two alone and *Timor mortis*
gone away. Is tendered breasts
and o how I have longed, my dear.

You do not like me, I know that.
You read my thoughts, you know I
cannot move; am sold with selling,
bought with buying, chained in lies.
I see them in your dry young eyes.
I am the doomed, the dying race.
When I hired you, I hired all
the Eumenides in one small face.

John Clare

First violets by the west field wall:
Not all in vain, not all the vile
Misunderstandings of little men
Made blind by a quickset accent,
A prickly self-esteem, an ignorance
Of commas, colons ... you were no
Orthographer. But still you knew
Ten thousand of their city minds
Could not begin to see you clear.
Your eyes, your tongue, your green
Fertility and voice.

Your eyes, not mine: your heart,
Not mine; your calloused hands,
Not mine. Eternally to you,
These violets by the west field wall.

You also broke the land too soon;
And made the rest seem all too late.

Crabbing

The sun just risen, the moon still high,
And nothing but the morning's birds,
The gulls, the redshanks, razorbills
Beneath the pale young summer sky –

These birds, the windless air and sea:
Quicky, his mate, my nephew and I
Chug westward to the wooded shore
In outward peace and honesty.

We stop and start and slowly haul
The wicker pots. Upward they float
Ribbed from the sea's translucent depths.
Hove on the deck the brown crabs crawl

Each osier cell. Then Quicky's skill:
Catching them neatly through the mouth,
The massive claws bent back just so,
He nicks and cuts. They soon lie still,

Baffled by all this light and death,
Ligaments severed, pincers vain.
I watch my nephew's knife-fixed stare,
His six-years-old of bated breath

As each spiked monster joins the rest.
He may relive them in his dreams,
As I did once, and wake one night
To face his sanity's first test

As scuttling horrors throng his bed.
I dreamt this many times when young:
That I was drowned, the world was drowned,
Only my flesh and the crabs not dead.

I touch his hair, but not for that.
I think how he, when he is old,
Will make a bitter judgement throne
Of this benched gunwale where he sat,

Since time must teach him that this dawn
Held something that we hid from him:
How his had been a shadowed year
In which no lucky child was born.

He must remember us with rage,
We three men on a dying sea
Who saw the oil and slicks of scum,
All the foul poison of their age

Filmed out around them like a pus,
Yet told him why the crabs got caught
Was out of stupid greed for bait.
We said they hadn't brains, like us.

Today he nods, and takes our word –
But what will he do when he looks back
And sees how cancerous-blind we were,
How sick, how viciously absurd?

Greed never trapped us in its cage.
We never sat and watched time haul
Earth onward to its stifled end.
He *must* remember us with rage.

ANTONIA FRASER

Poem for My Partner

You're my two-hearts-as-one
Doubled into game.
You're my Blackwood,
You're my Gerber,
You're my Grand Slam, vulnerable,
Doubled and redoubled,
Making all other contracts
Tame.

The Argument

Like stallions, your anger sweeps across the plain.
In the marshes, desperate, I crouch low,
Sadly intent on what my spear can do.
My strike pierces your belly, and again.
Still your horses flow.
Who is the enemy?
Who can know?

ATHOL FUGARD

Six Haiku

Useless net of words . . .
Still free, the serene beauty
Of a twilight sky.

Spring has been announced . . .
A silent gong of ripples
Where the swallow skimmed.

Lucky night-borne midge
Crawling across 'yesterday' . . .
The ink is dry.

Wagtail and a worm . . .
This summer has also fed
My forty-ninth year.

Did you also relish
The little butterfly's beauty
Fledgling Wagtail?

Gentle midnight breeze . . .
Compassionate sigh
At the end of a mantra.*

* Reference to the two-syllabled 'so-ha' at the end of certain Buddhist mantras.

ALAN GARNER

R.I.P.

A girl in our village makes love in the churchyard.
She doesn't care who, but it must be the churchyard.
They say she prefers the old part to the new.
Green granite chippings, maybe,
Rankle. Worn slabs welcome.
And after, in her bedroom,
She sees the mirror's view
Of her shoulder embossed
In Loving Memory.

Ann, why do you do it, you've eight O Levels?
Why not, Ann? If bones remember, you'll give them joy.
It's as good a place as any,
Close by nave, rood screen, chapel of ease,
Peal of the bells,
Bob Singles and Grandsire Doubles,
And when you half close your eyes,
The horned gargoyles choose.

But it has to happen.
Oh, Ann, tonight you were levelled.
William Jones, late of this parish,
Was cold beneath you, and his great-great-grandson
Warm above; and you rose,
Though your shoulder didn't know it,
In Glorious Expectation of the Life to Come.

STELLA GIBBONS

Coverings

The snake had shed his brindled skin
To meet the marching feet of spring.
With bar, curve, loop and whirling ring
The patterned swathes, papyrus-thin
Lay on the cage's sanded floor
Marked with dragging python-spoor.

Flick-flack! Like ash or vulcanite
His lidless eyes in the spatulate
Head were alive with watchful light,
Daring the sounds and the raw spring light.
He shone like watered silk from his tongue
To his tapering tail where the skin-shreds hung.

The cloudy yellow of mustard flowers
Was barred on his skin with jetty flares
And the five-patched circle the leopard wears;
The seashell's convolute green towers
Were called to mind by his belly's hue
That faded to pallid eggshell blue.

He was covered so to face the sun
That shadows of leaves might match his skin;
That where the lily roots begin
You might not tell where the snake begun;
That Man might see, when Snake was dressed,
God in Snake made manifest.

Mrs Fand wore a fox round her wrinkled throat.
He was killed at dawn as he snarled his threat
In a bracken brake where the mist lay wet.
Two men were drowned in a shattered boat
Hunting the whale for the silk-bound shred
That balanced her bust with her henna'd head.

An osprey plume brushed her fallen chin
And a lorgnette swung on her platinum chain
To deputize for her sightless brain.
Her high-heeled shoes were of python skin,
Her gloves of the gentle reindeer's hide,
And to make her card-case a lizard died.

She watched the flickering counterplay
As the snake reared up with tongue and eye
Licking the air for gnat or fly
And shook herself as she turned away
With a tolerant movement of her head –
'The nasty, horrid thing!' she said.

Ahmed

Ahmed the elephant
Wanders alone
In a green forest
By a mountain throne.

His ponderous feet
Through the marshland splay,
His trunk can scent
The breaking day
Or pick a leaf
From the highest spray,

And his brow can press
The sapling down
Till its soft white roots
Lie with its crown.

Though he roam at will
His vast green den,
Known is Ahmed
To the world of men.
By signed decree
They may hurl no spear
At the soft place hidden
Behind his ear,
Nor may the blunt
Blind bullet fly
At his wise, long-lashed
Ancient eye.

Alone to roam
Of eyes unseen
The misty forest
Strong and green
To pull the golden
Unreaped hay
Of silent, sun-bleached Africa –
Safe by decree
From the world of Man –
Lord, that I lived
As Ahmed can!

'Here Lies One Whose Name was Writ in Water'

Inscription on the tombstone of John Keats,
in the Protestant Cemetery in Rome

What stronger rune to be written in? –
Seething or locked in arcane permafrost.
Sans water Man would shrunken be and lost;
His very substance is of water made –
Of water and of dust.
Within its cloudy depths, secret and warm,
Shapeless and colourless his primal shade –
A pulsing jelly – strengthened into form.
Three days he can exist without the thin
Life-making flow. And music, in full streams,
Pours down all hills, giving voice to dreams.

Sweet boy! Bright star eclipsed at twenty-five
Your genius chose a metaphor too humble –
Water shall run while Earth herself's alive –
Iron rust, stone crumble.

VICTORIA GLENDINNING

Bloomsbury Barn Dance

On lilac evenings in Tavistock Square
High cultured voices hang in the air.
Bloomsbury's ghosts are gathering there.

Is there a stirring, a sense of unease?

Oh, see me do the Charleston,
The Rodmell, Crichel, Sissinghurst and Ham Spray,
The Garsington and Gordon Square dance.
Lord! what fun – as Mrs Woolf would say –
For all the biographers and lecturers and scholars
Generating interest and thesises and dollars,
Editions, annotations, treatises and texts,
Marketing the product with a flash of sex.
Gossip from the archives about literary buggery,
Sentiment and semen and sensational skullduggery,
Significant Form and the place of the arts
And a smatter of chat about private parts.
Spooning Apostles put terrible strains
On their Omega hearts and their Alpha brains.
When pacifism, feminism, civilization
Was noticed in the *T.L.S.* and argued in the *Nation*,
Discussed in their reviews and settled in their leaders,
They might not have envisaged quite so many Common Readers.
Bloomsbury groupies have grown so adept
At building careers from the papers they kept –

Roger, Vanessa, Duncan and Clive,
Lytton, Virginia, Leonard and Desmond,
Morgan and Maynard, Raymond and Dadie,
And anyone at all so long as she's a lady.
Interpreting, investigating, cerebrally masturbating,
Vicariously intimate and falsely familiar,
The Bloomsbury buffs get sillier and sillier.
With a hey and a ho-ho-Hogarth
And a nonny nonny no more please.

It's just the moon, and the wind in the trees ...

Or a Bloomsbury sneer and a Bloomsbury stare,
A Bloomsbury sigh and a chill in the air
On lilac evenings in Tavistock Square.

The Divorcee's Letter

'After a year, there's not a day that ends
without some thought of you.' Old days, old ways,
old rights, old rites, old talk, old friends
and old serenities; old scores, old strains,
old sores, old silences, old pains
and old constraints. 'Although I proved untrue,
the ideal me cleaves to the ideal you.'
They barely met – divided not by tears
but barriers, suspicions, babies, fears,
resentments, secrecies. They left behind
the gifts they had of blood and heart and mind
unwrapped, untapped, for newcomers to find.
Glad to be now inhabited, to give and live
again, away from him, she asks him to forgive
failure for which she cannot make amends.
'After a year, there's not a day that ends

without some thought of you. The other night
I dreamt that wordlessly you held my hand,
and in the dream we were at last all right.'
She cannot hope his own best dreams are so;
it's only that she needed him to know,
so that perhaps one day he'd understand.

RUMER GODDEN

Sonnet of Companionship

I walked with Wordsworth all this afternoon,
But not beside his lake; beside my river.
It was no season – March, November, June –
No century nor time, but mine for ever.

There was a fresher beauty in the fronds
Of willows falling, in the springtime light,
On ice glazed thick and dark on country ponds,
In summer's haze, in autumn's clear delight.

It was more simple than I had supposed.
We talked of dahlias, cottages and bees,
His happiness to read, as he composed,
To Dorothy as she sat shelling peas.

Another sound went with us as we talked;
Archangel wings that rustled as he walked.

The River

Because I know of other things
prescient in my spirit,
the light of summer evenings,
cool grass, the pleated wings
of swans, green water where the big barge glides,
roses and castles on its sides,

That painted rose was here and gone again
a hundred times, and I inherit
the prow, the passage and the wake; a stain
of shadow passes; castles in Spain
are burned upon the swan.
The river is a mirror, reflecting on and on.

Miss Midget

For Eva la Gallienne's Miniature Yorkshire Terrier

Is this
Miss?

A midget
fairy-bitch:
fidget,
wisp and witch
a quick, unique
minutia,
her tail can speak,
her ears can fly.

No darling, honeyed milk,
she blows now hot, now cold,
blent like her coat of silk:
mild silver, furious gold,
and, though her measurements are elf,
she is the whole world – to herself.

But earth needs heaven and she still
keeps vigil on the window sill;
listening, through wheels and steps, for One
Who is her moon, her stars, her sun.

WILLIAM GOLDING

Epitaph for My Accountant

Chryses, who had much paper filled,
Was by his falling papers killed.
He might have made his basement bulge
With secrets he could not divulge,
But chose to take a chance instead
And keep them stacked above his head.
Accountancy (a blameless thing)
Became his final reckoning.

Accountants who should chance to hear
This story do not drop a tear,
But always keep your attics clear.

Winter Night, 1945

This prison of the dark is wild with tears,
With agonies and tortured questioners,
With voices of the murdered, the half-dead,
Of lost and piteous children sick for bread.

Sleep easy and sleep quiet, prosperous man,
Only the innocent hold out their hands.
Time killed your heart long since and you can hear
Not so much noise as when tall grasses stir.

Τὸ Παιδίον

I read the book you could not understand.
You squatted on the beach to build in sand
A hollow, pointed shape and there beside,
Mounds to confront that sea without a tide.

Thin arms, pale hair, voice like a wren's, short dress
Of olive-grey and worked with crocuses:
Your hands were fumbling at a ship and all
The colonnades of Troy before her fall.

Sophocles, the Eminent Athenian . . .

Sophocles, the eminent Athenian,
Gave as his final opinion
That death of love in the breast
Was like escape from a wild beast.
What better word could you get?
He was eighty when he said that.
(Twenty-five more years
Of blood, sweat, toil and tears!)
For Ninon de L'Enclos,
When asked the same question said no.
She was uncommonly matey
At eighty.
And I?
        When I die
Heap rocks over me for what rest I can have,
Let concrete cover me.
Girls, keep off my grave.

L. P. HARTLEY

Candle-Mass

The conversation waned and waxed.
I was there; *you* were there.
Doubtless a few were overtaxed:
Talking was more than they could bear.

The aura of each candle-flame
Excited me, excited you.
I felt you in cach diadem;
Now in the yellow, now the blue.

The conversation waxed and waned:
Question, reply; question, reply.
We, for our intercourse, disdained
Such palpable machinery.

Columnar in transparent gloom,
Symbolical, inviolate,
Those candles held the spell of some
Campanile or minaret

That still takes in, as it exhales
The mood of joy or orison;
With hoarded ceremonials
Enfranchising communion,

Till every spoken word or thought,
However alien or profane,
Becomes the medium and resort
Where spirits spirits entertain.

So, idle talk's quintessences
Gleamed in the candles' radiance
With gathered stores of unproved bliss;
The multiplied inheritance

Of each succeeding moment . . . More
Perfect in form the flames appeared:
Their arduous stirrings overbore
Slight, wayward wisps that swayed and veered.

They changed their contours, one and all,
Carefully, persistently,
With efforts economical
That had their will of you and me.

For we somehow were party to
The issue of their enterprise;
Confounded in their overthrow,
Triumphant in their victories.

The alternation of each flame,
Thinning here, swelling there,
Compelled our souls into the same
Compass, ampler or narrower.

We knew that when those luminous spires
At last burned steadily and true,
(Our joy fulfilled with their desires)
We should have nothing left to do

But, self surrendered, acquiesce:
The promised consummation
Would drown our wills in its excess
And mingle both our souls in one.

When suddenly a permanence –
A flutter of wings before rest –
Drew down to those flame-forms: our sense
Was steeped in it, folded, caressed.

A casual, devastating gust
(The jolt, the sickening recoil!)
Our universe in chaos thrust;
And, not content to spoil

Our husbanded endeavour, threw
A mocking, flickering light,
Devoured by shadows, on us two.
The talk became more bright.

We entered into it with zest:
Question, reply; question, reply;
And lookers-on were much impressed
By our inane garrulity.

Yesterday

Like a timid child you were, Yesterday,
Whom the sun dragged out too soon
   And forced to play.
'Let me linger with the moon!'
   I heard you say.

I was insolent, I own, Yesterday,
When all blushingly you came
   A call to pay.
You slipped your dazzling card beneath the blind
   And let it fade away.

You left another one behind
   And let it stay.
And now I can't forget your name,
    Yesterday!

'He is only small,' I thought – yesterday.
   'Let him wait; he must be taught
   Better manners; no one ought
     To call this time of day!'
Did it shock you when I swore:
'Pull the blind down more – still more!'
   Then turned over with a snore
    And drowsed an hour away?

All your diffidence was gone, Yesterday.
   Innocence and youth had flown;
   Not a tree, not a stone,
    Not a flower
   But felt your power
When you swaggered through the noon-tide hour
   And seemed to say,
'Now I know a thing or two;
   A whisper here and there from you;
   Others by the way.
You look tired. A drink would do
   – If you care to pay.'

It was long ere evening came,
   The eve of yesterday.
I had wallowed deep in shame.
   You led the way.
I heard you as an ogre gaunt
Reiterate the dreary vaunt
'My bondsman thou for aye!'
   'No, no,' I muttered fast.
   'Thy dominion cannot last.
   Thy time is overpast.
Midnight has struck, and 'tis Today.'

'Fool! Fool!' I heard you say.
'I am not Yesterday.
I am his ghost that midnight cannot lay:
   Nor you, though you should pray
   Day after day.
   You who turned me
   From you, spurned me,
Now you are mine alway.'

The Door

'There is the door,' they whispered. 'There!'
(As if I did not know.) 'Take care;
It's rather steep. Four steps!' And then
They vanished down the sudden stair.

The door I stood before was small,
And nestling deep within the wall.
Athwart the door a shadow lay.
Bond-servants to the hour of day
Its goings and its comings were.
I could not see the little knot
That marred the smooth, white paint; forgot
How trivial the thing may be
That gives the lie to memory,
Whose flowers all fade if one doth die
And scentless leave the air.

But when the door – as though in sympathy
Interpreting the pressure of my hand,
Albeit irresolute and fugitive –
Swung open willingly and let me stand
Where lately I had longed, yet feared, to be,
The leaping fiend for joy imperative
Died in my heart. For everything breathed joy;

The dappled sunlight playing on the wall;
The sharp-peaked jasmine leaves, now staid, now coy,
With shadows dim grown ludicrously tall.
But most of all,
Marjoram, lavender and rosemary,
Their storied scents untying
And with the intruding honeysuckle vying,
Reconciled youth with memory.
I questioned not what incense this, what shrine.
The moment wept for, waited for, was mine.

Lost Illusions

(*Written in dejection*)

Why do I sit here all forlorn,
Watching the other kittens play,
Idling the sunny hours away,
Indolent, unamused, distrait,
    This fair September morn?

I was the foremost of them all
In daring games that kittens love;
And oft, my sovereignty to prove,
Would climb to branches far above
    The perilous garden wall.

In every leaf I saw a bird
And hunted it with might and main;
For hours I've watched a hole in vain,
And gone, and come and watched again:
    And now it seems absurd.

I loved the grasses that grew high,
Yet softly bent beneath my paw.
The longest, juiciest I saw,
I pounced on them and ate them raw:
    But now I pass them by.

There is a sameness in the air.
A sameness broods o'er everything.
My life is poisoned with its sting
And every joy has taken wing,
    Leaving me to despair.

I feel a change, a change in me.
I do not often want to purr.
I've grown neglectful of my fur,
In all things less particular,
    Sunk in a lethargy.

Will no one give me back the key,
The secret of my golden hours,
When I would even play with flowers –
Things that a coarser cat devours –
    Or is it lost to me?

No longer need the blackbird start
And rattle noisily away,
Clanging his warning where he may
To birds that erstwhile were my prey.
    For hunting I've no heart.

I am the only thing that grieves.
The other creatures do not care.
So to the forest I'll repair.
If Robin Redbreast finds me there,
    He'll cover me with leaves.

To a Blue Dragon

O great blue dragon, gaping terribly,
The potter's captive, narrowly confined,
What was thy sin that he should torture thee
    Time out of mind?
What was the fault that cost thee liberty?

Perhaps thine appetite laid China waste,
Battened on Manchus and on mandarins;
Tried if the maidens there were sweet to taste.
    Celestial sins!
Thy fury's frozen now, thy pride abased.

No more thy claw-prints in the yellow slime –
Purlieus through which the fickle Yangtsze flows –
Shall scare the lonely traveller: thy sublime,
    Tremendous toes
Are poised unclenched until the end of time.

Some stalwart of the base-born Kubla's reign
Slew thee, perchance, to win a king's reward;
And, awe-struck at thine antic shape, was fain
    With magic sword
To prick thee, ugly rogue, in porcelain.

Cramped into two dimensions, and denied
Subtle perspective's balm for outraged coils,
With half thy body spilling down the side,
    Thy blue blood boils
To feel thy symmetry so parodied.

Poor monster! Merchandized by sordid men,
Maimed as thou art, thou ne'er shalt leave my shelf.
I will not harbour thee awhile and then
    Sell thee for pelf.
Take heart, and make my cabinet thy den.

WILLIAM HORWOOD

Fifty Years Ago Today

Two kids
Shoving in a coffee bar
Pushed a frail old grubby dear
Fumbling at her tea and cake.
She had a soft, creased look,
An inturned mouth
And violet-lidded eyes.
She wore a thirties frock
She could have got in a jumble sale.
'Sorry,' they said
With barely hid contempt.

A dapper, dark-suit man,
Who had more money at his breast
Than she got in a month,
Rose up and left his paper, read, behind.
Why should she read its tale
Of fifty years ago today?

    PIG STY GIRL: Father Jailed
    The Society for the Prevention of it
    Poked about on hearing
    The slow gossip:
    What they found made headline news
    That warranted a picture of the dirty place,
    With arrows pointing to the very spot
    Where she made her bed in filth.

In the proceedings that followed the farmer said:
'Our girl was always queer.
She had a way of cowrin' in unlikely spots.
Just to annoy us she did it, so I thrashed her.
She scared the other children
And chose the place
All by herself without my help.
Then one day she disappeared.
I poked about some
And found her with the pigs
In the pig sty.
She was wearing her best frock
She stole from the drawer.
That was the last straw.
"Right," says I, "You stay here."
My wife agreed.
Well, she scared all the children
And caused me and my wife a great deal of fuss.
But we fed her reg'lar.
I know that's so
Because I did it same time I did the pigs.'

The lonely, frail old lady
Giggled at the young girls' rudeness
And said, 'My dad would have thumped you.'
'Why don't he, then?' dared the girls, for a laugh.
'He's gone to jail,' she said.
Then she began to cry.
'Now look what you done,' said one.
'Here, love, take this,' said the other.
'That's a pretty frock,' said the first, and
'Sorry we was rude.'
'One day my dad'll come out and take me back.'
'Yeh, I 'spect he will,' they said,
Leaving money for her on the paper
Where that old story was.

She did not pick it up,
But looked down at her frock and grinned:
Enough to make you want to look away.

Dirty Weekend Fantasy

Cottage in the country, love,
Far from the madding crowd
YOU KNOW
With a motorway outside the door,
With a wink of the eye
And a clink of the ice
With a drink of gin
We shall rust like tin:
In a twink we'll quickly die.

Country at the weekend, sweet,
Apart from the push and shove
.... I WANT
A two-day rest from the five-day stress,
From the rest of my friends,
From the best of my pals,
From the rugby maul,
From the social call:
In a twink we'll quickly die.

Bedtime in my cottage, dear,
Leaving the rage behind
.... TO SLEEP
In the peace of this countryside time.
Where the corn crops blow,
Where the dry stone falls,
With the ageless day
I'll close my eyes:
In a twink we'll quickly die.

We've woken in the gutter bore
Where the dirty puddles flow
.... WITH YOU.
There isn't a drain to take the flow.
The muddles grow big
With each break of day,
With a fuddle of men
I lust all day
For a dream that will quickly die.

FRANCIS KING

Patient

Praying with resignation for the skill
Of needle, draught, pill,
Or for the comfort of another's touch,
For someone whom to clutch,
Though needle, draught, pill
And touch of probing hands may only kill.

Waiting with resignation for the hours
Of love, tears, flowers,
Until it is our lives we wish to spend
To gain this little end,
Though love, tears, flowers
Come only with the death of all our powers.

Listening through agonies of cold and heat
To clock, heart, feet
Moving unseen above the polished floor,
Until upon the door
There is a sudden beat
And patient and impatient surgeon meet.

Hermes Psychopompos

Two beds, one stripped and one on which he lies,
Hearing the rush of wind, the rasp of rain,
And everywhere the small, omnivorous flies,
And high above his head that darkening stain.

The stain spreads out and out. This storm will last
All through the night. The frenzied water slaps
The marble quay, from which no boat is cast.
Mist makes the mountain crumble and collapse.

Below, four figures huddle round a table.
The boatman ponders, then flings down his cards,
As though, in some remote, Illyrian fable,
A god-man scattered divinatory shards.

What does he read from them? A queasy tossing
Of wave on wave on wave, a thread tugged tight,
Then snapping, as the small boat braves the crossing
Out of this dark into a blaze of light?

The boatman smiles, while in the room above
A vision flickers of those spilled cards lying
Beneath a brutal hand; and all that love
Becomes a long-drawn agony of dying.

Pigeons

A dry, persistent click and palpitation
Of wings on wicker, claws that scrape
In dreams of flight above the brawling station,
A fettered surging upwards for escape.

All through the night a ceaseless susurration
Floats on the clank and clangour of the rails,
And still those dreams of flight and wild gyration
Pulse through a tangled mesh of beaks and tails.

Then, as their roof explodes, what exaltation!
The sunlight splits the mica of an eye.
A clap and clatter from their habitation
Of earthly soilure to the unsoiled sky.

Flight on and on, in tremulous elation,
Beneath an alien, iridescent dome,
Beads strung together on a sole sensation:
A craving for the prison still their home.

Breakdown

That was his dream. But at the breakfast table,
The bitter peel upon his tongue, it lacked
Its former spell of fairy-tale or fable.
'And that was it? Just that?' Her neat hands stacked
Each plate on plate and he munched on, unable
To focus dream into a daily fact.

A simple dream. A plate forever falling
Out of her nerveless grasp towards the floor,
No cause for fear and yet somehow appalling,
That constant fall from now to nevermore.
And 'Help me, help me!' he was calling
As it smashed down against his being's core.

Weeks later, while she stacks the plates, she muses
(The peel still bitter on his tongue): 'You seem
Just as you were.' And, yes, he has no bruises,
The plate preserves its hard, unbroken gleam.
'How did it start?' she asks. But he refuses
Again to live the falling of that dream.

R. M. LAMMING

Oh?

Really, there's so little to be said,
Because I know you've lied;
And of course you know I know;
And what's more, I know why
You've lied. So we sit, ex-
Tending to each other smiles,
And those say quite enough.
'Wrong of me!' your own concedes,
'But still a good deal easier
And totally in character,
You must admit! Besides,
You shouldn't have asked!' And my
Smile answers, 'Right! Oh,
Absolutely!'
                    Ample proof,
I should have thought, if we
Had need of any: you and I
Such true friends.

She Wrote and Told Him . . .

She wrote and told him all the latest news;
He wrote 'I love you' in reply;
Which she read out at breakfast time
And tartly laughed; she said,
'My love has no small talk. I think,'
Said she, 'his brain has given out.'
And thereupon wrote elegantly back:
'Why don't you tell me something?'

Next Year

Her eyes frighten me.
Fear speaks to fear
Out of them;
So we talk of plans
For holidays next year,
When she'll be out of them.

But –

If we had it out
That fortnightly expectations
Are the most
Doctors dare provide for her –
Would she settle back today
And die, regardless
Of the calendar?

Acknowledgements

What we say belongs
To snow-cold strangers,
Is nothing to us;
Scarcely worth
Our forgiving.
What we think and
More, what we feel
– These also aren't
Our own possessions,
But we belong
To them, and they
Like parents stand
At the good house door,
Beckoning and half
Rejecting us.

DORIS LESSING

Here

Here where I stand,
Here they have stood,
All with our flowering branches.

Behind us five locked doors.
Behind them snarl the beasts
That licked our hands before.

Dark it is, and dark.
Lord, how strange to bring me to this close!

They too have stood asking:
Who shut the doors?
Who taught our beasts to snarl?

Who, what brought me here?

If I stand here then,
Where the dark came close,
Then here must close the dark,
Yes, here the dark must close.

A Visit

Alturnun was in that time.
I saw it there.
Through silence of high forest shade
The young king rode in then.
Reined three black trotting mares,
Laughed in his round hide chair.
A quick, blond, crafty face –
A race like cats, he and his fierce, fair girls.
They laugh as the blood runs, of that I'm sure.
Kiss and kill in a hard thriving time.
I'd not have thought the small visit of a dream
Could start such power of longing
For the stones, leaves, beasts, waters, men,
Held in the sunny light of Alturnun.
Hard to get there.
I've done it, though,
Once, tricking my way between dead thoughts,
Yet the signs for miles around that place
Say Alturnun, and Alturnun.

The Islands

The legendary islands are all very well,
But too strong a blast from there can set you wondering
If it's angels or devils that hold them.
Small sniffs at a time, yes, that's the way,
While the saving hands tutor a child
Or set new plants to grow.

When life beats too strong,
Promising more than this mind guesses at,
An underdrag of lethargy succeeds,
Filling where light was opening
With sleep like dirty water.
Then my doctoring, my knowledgeable hands,
Smooth white sheets or draw a cover up.

Once I thought the daily adding of small act to act
Food for the dulling of the heart,
Griefs and violence being the proper diet of liveliness.
Now, held back in every breath from folly of extremity
By what must be done, the here,
As frontiers are held by patience after war,
The quiet friend enters as my time-taught hands
Mix bread and set a damaged house to rights.

A Small Girl Throws Stones at a Swan in Regents Park

O my swan, my charmer,
Moving unruffled on that reach of water
Where stop the ripples from my ten strong fingers,
'Come,' say the breezes around your head,
'For once a cold, high singing, rumour
Of swans that could be princes,
Caused even the marketplace to shut its noise in wonder –
Come, break with your wings in thunder
And climb to rarer islands with this prince's daughter.'

A white neck crooked like an arm akimbo:
A thin, unseeing eye reflects a limbo
Where never a song was flawed from silence.

You circle orderly the chilly reaches,
Your image whitely upside-down beside you.
O far too perfect swan, my charmer,
That voice you think you're deceiving me with is mine!

Hunger the King

A man is given a dozen words to say,
Hunger first, with cold its brother,
Give me give me give me
Through a school of pap and promises
Till, drilled to obedience,
Cold and hunger stand to serve
That great table spread for middle life.
And then how lovely the loving, the laughter
The swift hates, like fuel,
And all the gallant children who stammer
As they wait for their places at the board,
And lustre of leaves and sky saying yes!
Here is what you thought,
Delight earned by working, here it is,
As they too fall back outspent and known,
To serve patience and the slow-taking pain.

Now all the guests have gone.
And all the words are said?
All said, they were so few.
A man is given a dozen words to say.
Hunger last, still stronger than the cold.

C. S. LEWIS

Leaving For Ever the Home of One's Youth

You, beneath scraping branches, to the gate,
At evening, outward bound, have driven the last
Time of all times; the old, disconsolate,
Familiar pang you have felt as in the past.

Drive on and look not out. Though from each tree
Grey memories drop and dreams thick-dusted lie
Beneath; though every other place must be
Raw, new, colonial country till we die;

Yet look not out. Think rather, 'When from France
And those old German wars we came back here,
Already it was the mind's swift, haunting glance
Towards the further past made that time dear.'

Then to that further past, still up the stream
Ascend, and think of some divine first day
In holidays from school. Even there the gleam
Of earlier memory like enchantment lay.

Always from further back breathes the thin scent,
As of cold Eden wakenings on wet lawns;
And eldest hours had elder to lament
And dreamed of irrecoverable dawns.

No more's lost now than that whose loss made bright
Old things with older things' long-lingering breath.
The past you mourn for, when it was in flight,
Lived, like the present, in continual death.

Finchley Avenue

We're proud of Finchley Avenue; it's quiet there,
High up and residential and in wholesome air,
With views out over London, and both straight and wide,
Shaded with copper beeches upon either side
Growing in grass, and corporation seats between.
There, as you walk, the houses can be hardly seen;
Such living walls of laurel and of privet stand,
Or sometimes rhododendron, upon either hand,
And once a wooden paling; and, above all these,
The amateurs and idlers of the world of trees –
Acacia and laburnum or such coloured things
As buzz and trill with birdsong and with insect wings.
Or else there may be banks of grass that steeply climb
Up to the hedge – reminders of the vanished time
When between fields this roadway ran of old the same
Straight course, and farmers called it by some different name.
    Even at the wooden gates if you look in you see
But little, for the drives are twisted cunningly.
A gravelled sweep, a shrubbery, a slope of grass,
A gable-end, is all they show you as you pass.
But you and I are privileged and, if we please,
May enter. We were cradled in such homes as these.
    Dating from nineteen-hundred or from nineteen-six,
They are steep-roofed, unstuccoed, and reveal their bricks;
By now they are out of fashion, and their very shape
And Tudorish graces damned with the black word Escape;
The bird-bath and the rockery and the garden seat
Scorned as a craven bourgeoisie's unearned retreat,
Whose privacy confesses a dim sense of guilt;
But all that looked so different when they were built!
These are your true antiquities. That garden lawn
Is the primordial fountain out of which was drawn
All you have since imagined of the lawn where stood
Eve's apple tree, or of the lands before the flood.

That little clump of trees (for it looks little now)
Is your original forest and has taught you how
To think of the great wilderness where trees go on
For ever after trees up the wild Amazon.
In that suburban attic with its gurgling sound
Of water pipes, in such a quiet house, you found
In early days the relics of still earlier days,
Forgotten trumpery worn to act forgotten plays,
Old books, then first remembered, calling up the past
Which then, as now, was infinitely sweet and vast.
There first you felt the wonder of deep time, the joy
And dread of Schliemann standing on the grave of Troy.
    The Avenue is full of life from nine till ten;
The owners of these houses are all hurrying then
To catch their trains. They catch them, and when these are gone,
By ones and twos the tradesmen in their vans come on;
The bread-man and the butcher and the man from Gee's
Who brings you soap and Rinso and a pound of cheese.
But even these come rarely after twelve, and soon
We sink to the dead silence of the afternoon.
    No countryside can offer so much solitude.
I have known the world less lonely in a winter wood,
For there you hear the striking of a village clock
Each hour, or the faint crowing of a distant cock.
But here is nothing. Nobody goes past. No feet
But mine. I doubt if anyone has used this seat,
Here in the shade, save only me. And here I sit
And drink the unbroken silence and reflect on it.
    What do they do? Their families have all gone hence,
Grown up. The whole long avenue exhales the sense
Of absent husbands, housework done, uncharted hours . . .
Is it painful emptiness that dully lowers
Over unhappy women – or a blessed state
Of truancy wherein they darkly celebrate
Rites of some *Bona Dea* which no man may see?
I am sure they are all virtuous, yet it seems to me
Almost an eerie rashness to possess a wife
And house that go on living with their different life,

For ever inaccessible to us, all day;
For, as we knew in childhood, if the fathers stay
At home by chance, that whole day takes a different tone,
Better, or worse, it may be; but unlike its own.

Hermione in the House of Paulina

How soft it rains, how nourishingly soft and green
Has grown the dark humility of this low house
Where sunrise never enters, where I have not seen
The moon by night nor heard the footfall of a mouse,
Nor looked on any face but yours
Nor changed my posture in my place of rest
For fifteen years – oh how this quiet cures
My pain and sucks the burning from my breast!

It sucked out all the poison of my will and drew
All hot rebellion from me, all desire to break
The silence you commanded me. . . . Nothing to do,
Nothing to fear or wish for, not a choice to make,
Only to be; to hear no more
Cock-crowing duty calling me to rise,
But slowly thus to ripen laid in store
In this dim nursery near your watching eyes.

Pardon, great spirit, whose tall shape like a golden tower
Stands over me or seems upon slow wings to move,
Colouring with life my paleness, with returning power,
By sober ministrations of severest love;
Pardon, that when you brought me here,
Still drowned in bitter passion, drugged with life,
I did not know ... pardon, I thought you were
Paulina, old Antigonus' young wife.

DAVID LODGE

A Martian Goes to College

(*with apologies to Craig Raine*)

Caxtons are bred in batteries. If
you take one from its perch, a girl

Must stun it with her fist
before you bring it home.

Learning is when you watch a conjurer
with fifty minutes' patter and no tricks.

Students are dissidents: knowing
their rooms are bugged, they

Take care never to talk
except against the blare of music.

Questioned in groups, they hold their tongues,
or answer grudgingly, exchanging sly

Signals with their eyes
under the nose of the interrogator.

Epilepsy is rife, and the treatment cruel:
sufferers, crowded in dark and airless cells,

Are goaded with intolerable noise
and flashing lights, till the fit has passed.

Each summer there's a competition
to see who can cover most paper with scribble.

The sport is hugely popular; hundreds
jostle for admission to the gyms,

And must be coaxed out when
their time is up. A few, though,

Seem unable to play, and sit staring
out of windows, eating their implements.

Snow in Suburbia

Sunday in the city, and there is snow.
It melts reluctantly in cold canals;
Buses plough furrows through the heavy slush;
Congregations steam gently through the first hymn.

In the quiet, residential street
Few footsteps violate the white carpet.
A kind of grace has settled on
The roofs of ugly, half-timbered houses.

It softens the bulbous shapes of cars,
Clings delicately to clotheslines, privet hedges,
Moulds itself to heaps of coal,
Spends its beauty on the meanest object.

But behind the doors of 'Ferndale',
'Belmont' and 'Sunnyside' stand men
Gum-booted and breathing quickly, their hands
Eagerly fingering the handles of spades.

Scarcely has the snow begun to falter
Before they are out, and the street resounds
To the rasp and scrape of iron on stone.
They are turning the white beauty upside down

And hurling into the gutter,
Exposing the dirty pavement and the hard
Line of the kerbstones. This done,
They brush the tops of their gates and hedges.

Then, with tools at the ready, they march up the street,
Knocking on the doors of the aged, sick and widowed,
Offering to rid more paths and pavements
Of the intolerable white plague;

Until only one semi-detached house bears
Its spotless white apron. My house.
They look reproachfully at my front door,
For I am neither aged, sick, nor widowed.

Making a spyhole in the misted window,
I peer down at the desecrated street.
The men prowl round my apron, but will not touch it.
One is shaking the snow from a sooty tree.

Dissatisfied, the men disperse, stamping their boots,
Squinting at the sky, hopeful of another fall.
Satisfied, I return to my book.
I prefer my sepulchre whited.

Epitaph For a Film Star

Passing the hoarding where she was displayed,
From which destructive nails had peeled
Long, ragged strips of irregular depth,
(Breast and buttock in the gutter fade)
One glimpsed, beneath the wounds she smiled above,
Fragments of other images, appeals:
A baby's limb, a page half-turned,
Ban the – Save the – Dancing – Love.

Now eyes and speculation stick
Where nails have scraped through to the stark brick.

OLIVIA MANNING

Written in the Third Year of the War

The men that went out of Athens on the bright day in spring
When everyone had a flower or a flag, and the Greeks were carrying the
    bearded sailors,
Like classic heroes, aloft on their shoulders.
The men that went out that day waved from the lorries,
And when we cried 'Good Luck!' called back to us 'We're off to Berlin!'
Those that began returning a week later had nothing to say.
The clouds hung low, bagged with wet, and the wind stripped petals
    from the trees.
They stared with blank eyes over the lorry sides, the bandages muddy on
    their heads.
We watched with compassion and bewilderment.
It seemed a long way to bring the wounded. We were not told how close
    the Germans followed.
When the lorries stopped and the men slid down like old men, blind,
    without response for us,
We felt then a thing unknown to our generation, the sorrow and terror
    of defeat.

As we lay in the harbour amidst sunken ships,
Our decks crowded, the guns uptilted on the quayside,
The creeping sun for the last time lit for us
The Acropolis and its tokens of ancient wars.
Others were driven out before this; we had held ourselves an unbiddable
    people.

When the brilliance of the Peloponnese went down in darkness, when
    the night came between us,
Our friends returned to Athens, excited a little, more afraid. We faced
    the sea
Knowing until the day of our return, we would be exiles from a country
    not our own.
We, the deniers, have known long denial.
Alien in a domesticated land, choiceless between the century-planted and
    the sand,
We are a long way from childhood, from the wild shore and the mountain
    wind.
He who shared memory, he who awaited and recalled us, has died before
    we could return to him.

The future may lead elsewhere now. It will not matter.
Have we not learnt enough?
Separation become for ever has brought us low, and victory will have an
    emptiness.
There's not much spared us. Born into war and ignorant of peace, our
    arrogance
Grew from longing. In the end we may know a thing withheld us from
    our birth.

Black Cat

Hist, black and
Guilty-walking cat!
Each muffled paw bespeaks
A lust for fish.
Lean, secret, delicate,
Devourer in one mouthful
Of the dish;
Rapt and yet ready
To flash round;
Magical disappearer
At a sound!
What is your mystery?
Designed in body
For no greater vice
Than will to feed yourself,
Your sinuous silence
To beguile but mice.

ARTHUR MARSHALL

John Betjeman Celebrates the De-rationing of Sweets in 1954

There's nougat at the Hendersons',
The Hopes have got some fudge,
And Pam has popped the pralines
In the tool-bag of her Rudge.
Voluptuous and tarmac-borne
She free-wheels through East Cheam,
My caramelly angel-girl
My luscious sweetmeat dream.

Down bypass, heathland-hugging
Coasts my freckled, blazered bliss.
The long-awaited puncture
Brings the peardrop-scented kiss,
And butterscotchy handclasps
As we map our true love's course.
Sweet the pangs of adolescence!
Sharp the prickles of the gorse!

At dusk, through built-up roadways,
Bird-bath, loggia and gnome,
To geysers, brunch, elevenses,
The wonderland of home.
But who can think of Beauty,
Spare a thought for things Above,
When Oxshott's full of marzipan
And hearts are full of love?

NAOMI MITCHISON

Mauritian Landscape

The tail of the cyclone suddenly drags a veil
Over the peaks and jags that shimmer through:
Illustrations in faded ink of some old fairy-tale
Where only the lucky succeed, the many fail.
There were dragons up there that boiled and grumbled and flew
And bit off the hands and feet of fugitive slaves
From endless piling of rocks to clear for cane and more cane
To keep their elegant masters safely out of this rain
That blots the landscape into forgotten graves
Of all who came here to grab and kill and destroy,
Leaving so little beauty that atones
For the poor dear dodo's unlamented bones.
But the British came, moral and circumspect,
Their gentry manly and their virgins coy,
Quite unaware of aspects of neglect:
Dragon destroyers. What else did you expect?

Oldies

If you go sleeping happy on heathery places,
The ticks will be at you with their sharp embraces
Delightedly burrowing through zips and buttons and laces.

Best for us oldies to stay snug in our gardens,
Not try to meddle outside and get no pardons
From those whom a new hope or hate averts and hardens.

If you read too many memoirs and dream before sleeping,
Up jump those old worn-out hopes and ideas at you, bleeping
And digging up dead loves from what you had thought safe keeping.

Lyke-Wake

Oxford my heart ache, the young go by
With the pains and pleasures that make their must,
Shouldering ghosts from street to street:
Among them I,
Casting the dust, casting the dust from my feet.

Oxford once lay in golden air;
Wise and witty could argue and meet
In all their delicate cut and thrust.
But I was there,
Stirring the dust, stirring the dust with my feet.

For her lyke-wake nor proctor nor don:
Oxford, when earth's hard crust
Dissolves into fire and fleet:
(*Lord have mercy upon us*)
I shall be gone,
Lost in the dust, lost in the dust from my feet.

Midsummer 1956

Midsummer smoke goes high as Harwell,
Harwell chimneys that stand so high.
Icarus flies round Harwell chimneys,
Quietly falls from the midsummer sky.

Those who worship at holy Harwell
Will ride the world with a grasping grip,
But the White Horse with the bitless mouth
Can take no bridle, can take no whip:

Will bear no whip and will bear no rider,
Nor none will bear until time is done.
The sun stands higher than Harwell chimneys;
The White Horse is another sun.

JOHN MOORE

Draw Close the Curtains

Draw close the curtains. (Mares' Tails streaking the night sky
   And looks like rain?)
With the wireless going, you won't notice the creeper
   Rat-tatting on the pane.
Shut out the night with its wild whispering voices,
   Its cries and its calls,
The tempestuous world kept at bay with your solid
   Inviolate walls.
So settle down to a peaceful finish to Christmas.
   Kick off your shoes;
Cherry-logs merrily crackling, a drink at your elbow,
   Time for the News.
Cat on the hearth, book on your lap, and suddenly over the air,
   Out of the void, into your quiet,
   Come the great sea-names that roar and riot,
Humber, Lundy, Faroes, Forties, Fastnet, Forth and Finisterre!

Tendril of creeper beats a tattoo on the window
   Like a limed linnet.
Know now that you live on an island! – Your house is
   An island within it!
The pitiless winds of the world all about you; and surging
   Into your room
Comes the heave and the sigh and the crash of the steep Atlantic,
   The spray and the spume.
The fire leaps high, and harshly the dry logs sputter.
   The wind has risen!

The chimney always smokes when it's in that quarter. . . .
　　Islander, listen:
As the cat gets up and your book falls shut, and suddenly over the air,
　　Out of the void, into your quiet,
　　Come the great sea-names that roar and riot,
Humber, Lundy, Faroes, Forties, Fastnet, Forth and Finisterre!

JAN MORRIS

Pig Rhyme

A mother pig crooned to her sweet little piglets three:
Come, wipe all the mud from your trotters, and if you are good – we'll
see!
There *may* be a bucket of acorn swill for your tea!

Swill, said the piglets, acorn swill, oh wow!
Is that all you've got, you silly old sow?

The mother pig cried: But when *I* was wee,
A bucket of swill was oh, such a treat for me!
On birthdays I had it, and when I was good as could be!

Big deal, said the piglets three.

Four Cat Couplets

Move over, says the Cat, nine-tenths of the bed are mine.
Yes: in lives and comfort, the ratio's one to nine.

★

My Cat is Sleep made flesh and fur:
Is Death itself a purr?

★

Oh, oh, the crime of the claw, the Kraken eye!
It is only a game: may the best mouse die.

★

I watch through all th' Eternity of the Soul,
In case – in case – ah, Ecstasy! – the Heap gives forth
A Mole.

IRIS MURDOCH

Agamemnon Class 1939

In Memoriam Frank Thompson 1920–1944

Do you remember Professor
Eduard Fraenkel's endless
Class on the *Agamemnon*?
Between line eighty-three and line a thousand
It seemed to us our innocence
Was lost, our youth laid waste,
In that pellucid unforgiving air,
The aftermath experienced before,
Focused by dread into a lurid flicker,
A most uncanny composite of sun and rain.
Did we expect the war? What did we fear?
First love's incinerating crippling flame,
Or that it would appear
In public that we could not name
The aorist of some familiar verb.
The spirit's failure we knew nothing of,
Nothing really of sin or of pain,
The work of the knife and the axe,
How absolute death is,
Betrayal of lover and friend,
Of egotism the veiled crux,
Mistaking still for guilt
The anxiety of a child.
With exquisite dressage
We ruled a chaste soul.
They had not yet made an end

Of the returning hero.
The demons that travelled with us
Were still smiling in their sleep.

Heralded by the cries of hitherto silent Cassandra,
The undulating siren creates in the entrails
And in the heart new structures
Of sensation, the abrupt start
Of war, its smell and sound.
The hours distend with bombs,
The big guns vibrate in the ground.
Frightened men kill by remote control,
Or face to face, appalled, see their enemy fall.
Houses and public buildings with a kind of surprise
Bend their knees and turn into tombs.
Ever so many gentle worlds quietly end.
People sleep in catacombs.
White paths of doomed men
Daily criss-cross in the skies.
The sanctuary is bombed and lies
Open and unmysterious,
A garden of wild flowers.
Something crawls wounded on,
But the Holy One
Having suffered too long
Eventually dies.

Delphi medises and Apollo's face grows dim.
Was there a god there? We never saw him.
A priest was making a political sound.
Fey Helen lost her beauty and her shame,
Went home quite pertly in the end they say,
Piously helped the poor, became
A legend haunting a fought-over ground.
What was it for? Guides tell a garbled tale.
The hero's tomb is a disputed mound.
What really happened on the windy plain?
The young are bored by stories of the war.

And you the other young who stayed there
In the land of the past, are courteous and pale,
Aloof, holding your fates.
We have to tell you it was not in vain.
Even grief dates, and even Niobe
At last was fed, and you
Are all pain and yet without pain
As is the way of the dead.

No one can rebuild that town
And the soldier who came home
Has entered the machine of a continued doom.
Only the sky and the sea
Are unpolluted and old
And godless with innocence,
And twilight comes to the chasm
And to the sea's expanse
And the terrible bright Greek air fades away.

Too Late

What has she got left for her old admirer,
After a lifetime wed to the usurper?
When he was young he dreamed of being solitary;
The real aloneness later was another matter.
He needed then the thought of how she cried
At their brief meetings, and he carefully
Wrote the veiled letters which she not forbade,
Where high hopes hinted at were not denied.
His bright hair faded to a parching grey
And started to fall out. She never strayed;
Some cruder matters were not spoken of
In the long conversation of their love
Even their doubt was of obscure intent.

Death was not quick to take the thug away,
That death upon which they were both so bent
In a laconic upright sort of way.
(He thought, she's too discreet even to *pray*!)
Did he observe her sadness with some glee,
Savour the sense of her wild discontent,
Doleful and damned inside the situation?
Did guessing at her grief bring consolation
During his studied patience? Naturally he
Felt at her ruined life some satisfaction,
Could not be reasonably refused a gloat
About that ancient and disastrous error
Which she repented of over and over,
Her failure to choose this instead of that,
Which should have been dead easy! Yes, indeed,
Gloats he and checks, achieves no resignation.
Hard to remember now the early grace
Of love's unselfish rapturous elation.
Years passed in which he saw her lovely face
Lose all its quick response, grow desperate,
Thickened and slow, a sort of blinded look.
Grief is a secret worm, and even he,
He felt it crossly, was shut out.
Better perhaps. She would not later brook
What he might then have witnessed: better not to see.
Quite slowly she has made her terms with fate.
Her early charms disintegrate and sag.
She drinks a lot and has put on weight.
Objectively, she has become an old bag.
'Of course you're older, dear, but beautiful,
At least to me,' he tells a tearful smile.
Life is a matter of choosing, *ergo* of losing,
They formulate when feeling philosophical.
Thank God at least no bloody kids arrived,
Doubtless because. He keeps a tactful style,
A sort of grim ironical gentleness
Being the atmosphere in which they have survived.
Letters, occasional meetings near her home

In office hours, as if by accident,
No travelling, an always urban scene,
And public, as if that meant innocent.
He has died in those tea shops, later in bars.
(They have lived through quite a lot of social change.)
Oh God, he was so young when it began, how strange, how strange,
How worst of all that his own schemes
Were what destroyed his youth and his good looks
And his light heart and high I.Q.
And all those splendid dreams!
He might have written books, if she
Had been his wife, he would have made his mark;
Or if he'd had the sense to chuck her at the start,
And look for someone else, or just be free.
But vile emotions blocked his larger view
And early bafflement quite needlessly destroyed his life.
He turned to making money, even that
With only moderate success. His little flat
(To which she never came) is mean,
Provisional, just like a student's den.
Planning some final transformation scene,
He never bothered to try out his taste.
His hi-fi is unplayed, his books are chaste.
When all is makeshift art cannot bring peace.
At later times they talked about the south
And how they'd run away perhaps to Greece,
A place where tender veins of pebbles shine
In the still sea through deep transparent water.
At least in Maytime in an English field
To lie in buttercups he once besought her,
(The old swine being established as elsewhere
Fishing or something. Christ, he didn't *care*!)
To get away right out of London just for once
By car for half a day. She havered.
He ground his teeth and never quite forgave her.
Now he is testy, she apologizes.
Sometimes she would be sulky did she dare.
Their tragic story holds no more surprises.

He plays at leaving but can go nowhere.
At the longed-for last he has gained a ghost.
She timidly proposes this and that.
Can they start life anew? What life and how?
He stays on in his flat and wants no changes now.
Does he desire her? No. The welcome death
Emancipates, it seems, not her but him.
Even at this late hour he'll have some fun.
Now that his sacrifice is over and proved vain
He won't be fooled again, he's not yet done.
What is she crying for – her vanished youth?
I too was beautiful when I was young.
Or is she crying for that bloody man,
For her dead husband, for the real one?

Music in Ireland

While we are hearing Mozart in this barn
Rain clatters on the roof
Which is made of corrugated iron
Or some such stuff.
Mozart can manage all the same
To elevate the noisy rain
Into a delicate suspended dome
Or ceremonial tent with glittering fringes,
Making it very taut and still.
The barn is rather damp and chill
And people's clothes give off a cold steam
A somewhat awkward wet and woollen smell.
Afterwards there will be tea and scones
And dark blackcurrant jam
And a guided tour of the house.

We are in Ireland.
Murders are planned in time at certain hours
In homely kitchens when the meal is finished
By thoughtful men sitting beside turf fires
Over a drink with comradeship and wit
Especially at weekends when leisure comes
For planting bombs, the weekly labour done.
Monday will bring again
The breaking of the news to families,
The life sentence of the child witness,
The maimed beloved in the wheel chair,
The condemnation to unending pain, and tears
Which have nothing to do with Mozart.

Near by on Strangford Lough
Migrating geese bound for the Arctic Zone,
Stand solemnly upon the glossy mud
In the brown twilight of the afternoon,
Soon to move on toward the midnight sun
With empty hills of snow to walk upon,
But now are waiting, dignified and sad,
Big heavy birds obedient to God,
Closely observed by the local bird-watching society
Against a misty background of factory chimneys.

Murder is abstract, something not imagined
In detail or defined as such,
Negating love and mercy, hideous
Schema of a hating mind.
This music too is a material
That's not entirely human,
Instant and imageless as angels are,
Absolute in formation as the snow crystal,
Of necessity the aloof laughter,
Of undeserved delight the avatar,
Hinting the rhythm of the planet.

This is the matrix that we cannot fathom,
It is our response that is human,
Our restless yearning in the day's event
Our temporal desire for resolution,
Our confused sense of a before and after.

The music lifts like steam
The secret cares of hearers
Tired with cold and rain
And intermittent dream
Of their own sorrows and the old
Sorrows of Ireland,
Which they try to banish.
Heads bowed down or thrown
Backward open-eyed
Here and there are dark
With terrible deaf pictures.
Sounds rise up and vanish
Into a pitted dome.
It continues to rain.
The acoustics being imperfect some people fidget.

Something which is pure has come
To a high magnetic field.
Cry out as it passes on,
When shall we be healed?

John Sees a Stork at Zamora

Walking among quiet people out from mass
He saw a sudden stork
Fly from its nest upon a house.
So blue the sky, the bird so white,
For all these people an accustomed sight.

He took his hat off in sheer surprise
And stood and threw his arms out wide
Letting the people pass
Him by on either side
Aware of nothing but the stork-arise.

On a black tapestry now
This gesture of joy
So absolutely you.

ENOCH POWELL

Alexander

Alexander, Alexander – I saw him die.
Not in the hanging gardens of the East,
By the slow Tigris, in the pillared hall
Thronged with his Macedonian soldiery
Long ages gone; but here, this hour, close by,
The living Alexander, lord of all,
Suffered and died; and I, of men the least,
Have seen the destined saviour of mankind
Suffering, dying, and done naught to save,
Have neither spoken word nor uttered cry,
Nor sought for his to cast my life away.
God, God, forgive me, miserable me!
For what am I, that I could save or slay
The conqueror of the world? But oh, I feel
He will not hear me. He will not repeal
My curse; I am condemned until the grave
To bear the torture of my guilty mind.

Os Lusiadas

[In October, 1559, the Portuguese poet Luís de Camões, then aged thirty-five, was shipwrecked at the mouth of the Mekong river while being carried as a prisoner from China to India. He saved his life by swimming ashore, bringing with him nothing except the seven completed cantos of his *Lusiads*, the great national poem celebrating Vasco da Gama's discovery of the sea route to India. Though destitute, he contrived to reach Goa at some time before 7 September 1561. By 'poetic licence', the author has transferred the scene from Cambodia to Timor.]

Black the mountains of Timor,
　　Sweeping from the sea,
Watched Camoëns drift ashore,
　　Rags and misery.

Warm and heavy from the East,
　　A wind that rose and sank
Like the breathing of a beast
　　Landward bore the plank.

Softly playing forth and back,
　　Breakers ringed the bay,
Till the huddled shape of black
　　Broke the line of grey.

Then he stirred, and up the sand
　　Crawled, too weak to walk,
Holding in his battered hand
　　A jointed fennel-stalk.

Hidden in that hollow rod
　　Slept, like heavenly flame
Titan-stolen from a god,
　　Lusitania's fame.

Transubstantiation

Be the priest evil, by the herd
Of worshippers the doctrine unbelieved,
Yet, at the word
And magic deed
The miracle achieved,
The lifeless lives and feels and bleeds
And is through pain
A sacrifice again,
Rising immortal from mortality,
Unspotted from profane,
And pleads
For who naught heed.

And though thou wert
False and thy meaning mockery
And I, by thee
And by myself deceived,
Wrought my own hurt,
Yet was not vain
The consummating act
Of our unspoken,
Made nor broken
Pact,
Which in that instant drawing breath
Immortal flew,
Subsisting separate,
Untrammelled by our fate,
And in a life beyond our death
Now intercedes
For mercy on us two.

Asthma

I stir, and in the darkness hear the noise
That must have waked me – steady, rhythmic notes,
A high one alternating with a low.
The sounds are known to me; their cause is breath
That fights a passage through the tightened ducts
And strangled orifices of the lungs.
Now, wide awake, I lean upon one arm
And stare into the dark, as though my stare
Could pierce the night and show me what I know:
The form propped up in bed, the arching chest,
The dull, dishevelled hair, the starting eyes.
Backwards and forwards, like an idle bow
Drawn across fiddlestrings, the sound vibrates;
Backwards and forwards moves the unseen bow
Across my heartstrings, till I turn and cry
In agony of utter helplessness.
This narrow space that separates our beds
Seems the dark cavern of eternity,
Through which we grope alone, but suffering
By the imagination of a state
External to us. That strange destiny
Which makes one thing impossible to man
Of all things most desired, by word or act
To help another, has condemned us here,
Lying a yard or two apart, to weep
In uncommunicable loneliness.

JEAN RHYS

I Buy Your Dreams

I am a clerk, spectacled, flat-footed, growing old,
Earning three-ten a week;
Not one of the conquerors;
One of the lowly ones . . .

But I dream, my masters, I dream.
All creatures dream.
A wild and misty liberty
On which you lay no hand — or so you say.

Yes, by your kind permission, I have my dreams . . .

(Of the time when I'll get my hand on your necks and
tear your throats out, revenge myself for twenty years of
eating mud? Not so. That's an exaggeration.)

I dream the dreams you give me, masters:
Of paying off my 'easy terms';
Conducted rambles for my holidays;
Football, and getting drunk on Saturday.
Sometimes I take a flight and dream of luscious film-stars,
Smart restaurants, cars that break records . . .

And then wake, snarling . . .

To dream again of film-stars,
Murders, thefts . . .

(One of my kind has dared, one of my kind.
They've got him, and he gets five years' hard.
Hurray, I think, they've got him!
Why should others escape from the trap that I am in?)

I grow old, my masters, dreaming the dreams you give me,
Dreaming, by your kind permission, of film-stars,
Murders, Monte Carlo, asters in my garden . . .

If I should think?
                But that's
                    What you try
                        So hard
                            To stop.
                                Don't you?

PAUL SCOTT

'I, Gerontius –'

A TRILOGY

The Creation – The Dream – The Cross

THE CREATION

I

If we consider the ends
the ends leading to the greatest end
and the greatest end ending for ever
If we consider Life

Let it be said we consider
all things all things considered
by us and all things to us
inspirations to the great end

Then we consider nothing
or considering nothing can
be nothing to us for ever
then Nothing attained

Nothing attained Nothing
Desolate is the cry and great the shoutings
accompanying this void
this empty masquerade of living

I saw many masks in the moonlight
striving to attain the moon

II
There is a corner of earth
earth's corner dusty uncared for
corner of earth we know

Great are the works of thy people
O Lord God of Hosts
They sweep through the Bright Cities
and toward the Plain of Sodom

Let there be rejoicings
O Lord God of Hosts
Thy people are great in their works
Glorifying Thee in Eternity

The Great Exodus is upon us
upon us is the Great Void
the emptiness and the lamplight
and the worn cat in the corner

Into the East drone the great planes
where the West is reflected
Carrying Thy words in their voices
O Lord God of Hosts

O Tumultuous cities of the dazzling plains
Great is Thy Glory and great Thy Brightness
Defend for ever Thy Greatness in loud voices
Lest another cry come unto us!

REQUIEM

III
How deep are thy waters Ladoga
how still? The snows of Narvik
are broken with great voices
Pharaoh! Thy tomb is Namsos

Silently they march in the moonlight
likening the hard white bones to snow
How far to Canaan Children?
O! Children of the snow
How far how far? Then forward
to Helsinki they go

IV

My heart dries with the summer
throbbing dull passionless notes
dragging wearied memories through
the avenue of limes
My Children!
My Children!

O Great are Thy works my Children!

V

See you the crowded cities?
Hear you the frightened voices?
Feel you the hunger
and the sharp stinging pain
of hopelessness?

I must arise and go
and mingle with the crowd
laugh at Thy Sorrowed Face
and unheard pleadings

O! My Children!

Shows not the Lily in the water?
And the strange white heather
meadows voices?

Say 'I loved all these
but I forgot them
And madness has come unto me'

VI

I shall not pass unheard
along the unbroken lines
dragging old memories through the once fair city

They shall say of me
'That stone the corner one
he touched it as he passed along this way'

VII

And In The Beginning God Created
and if we consider the ends
the ends leading to the One Great End
and the Greatest End Ending Forever
Let us consider Life

THE DREAM

I

Dream on Gerontius! dream
and dreaming you will dream no more
Such as I Gerontius know not you
nor knowing you will pass you in
the street

I walked alone in the vineyards
of Naboth and Naboth met me
under the first vine and cried aloud
to me 'Stranger this is no vineyard
but your Soul!'

And I saw my Soul detach itself
from the first vine and press grapes
to my parched lips and Naboth
went and I never saw him more
only my soul in the first vine
                    I cry 'Vine!

you know me as I stand naked
but unashamed?'
                    and the vine
shrunk its greenness into my eyes
becoming dull and painful to me
that I cried again 'Vine!'
                    and I saw
no more the grape but the apple
which Eve plucked and it was on the
first vine and my Soul inherited
the wickedness of the earth

Dream on Gerontius! Amid the
Angels cast not out the vine
lest ye cast the wickedness of the
Earth from Heaven to my Soul!

II
I lay me down by a green pasture
and green was the land and the water
springing from the dull rocks was
green to my eyes

And the Jade of Confucius was
upon my neck and I had great
wisdom around my body
amid the green pastures

Then came the Graces to my side
and sang me asleep in the still noon
and I dreamed I saw Jesus
sitting upon the Right Hand of God
The Father
            Almighty
                    Upon
                        Heaven
                            and Earth

'Be as a child,' said Jesus unto me
and I was as a child and understood
not His words which were wise

And the green pastures became yellow
in the evening and I awoke
and I was alone alone
none was there and I was desolate
and cried in my great loneliness

And I was as a child no more
and remembered the words in
my dream but Jesus spake them not
but Gerontius dreaming of the first vine

THE CROSS

After the Temporal fall
the burning Voice of Spiritual Flame
leaps to the summit of Heaven
encrimsons the Word
The House the God
fires the lost Temporal power
which with phoenix wings
swoops to the ageless arms
of servitude enslaves the many
goads the great Divine
the Ultimate the Hope.
goading the pressing throng
into the hidden crevices of prayer
down the long darkness to Eternal nought
the End the Death
the Thought

How to conceive the Word
the flame the power
the needed blessing of the Sacrifice
How to conceive conceive
the day of Dread the End
Rebirth?

Burn the cool quenched lips
lips cool to the earthen hope
hope cooled to the flaming heart
the channel the soul
the soul bewailing the gloomed
tunnel of delight
the eternal reaching for the stars
the eternal night
Bring to the unhoped care
the care of hope the silver chalice
and the crimson wine
the flickering candle and the burning Eye
the swaying vestments swaying
in sleep and doubt
the whirr of heavy wings
about the flowered altar
the dreaming Christ-Child
and the Holy Wife
The Old Man moves

'Preserve thy body and soul
Unto Everlasting life'

Down the green tunnel of despair
the floating wings wings
sound of wings in the closed ear
Pressed to the covetous eyes
the fleshy hands

Everlasting Life

The Holy Breath breathes through
the motionless throng the prayer
low in the wooded aisle
echoing through the roof high
to the temporal eye
the Love the Death
The Cross
the Holy Sign of words wronged
by the wronging lips
betrayed in the silent night
betrayed in the silent night
and the three cock-crows
betrayed to Eternal Life the Nails
the Cross the Saving Blood

Promised by the Word the Word
to the land promised and the
Promised Land unhearing the
Promised Word

Was the way long and the burden
unbearable the pain of thong
the thorn the yielding Holy Flesh
pained in Eternal Life?

Did the brow sweat the eyes
close the dead world world
killed and world unknown
for ever and ever?

The Great Coming is upon us
since Calvary threatened
since the thudding wood
and the bleeding side the pale air
cut by the rearing Tree

The blossomless tree blossoming
Life out of Death and Death coming
before the promised Life
and Death saving the darkness
falling upon the land and the
weeping women women weeping
by the obscure cross on the Hill

How went the hours the hours
of death and the flaring up of the
endless hours of Life?

And in those hours these hours
come and go like children passing
a window and returning with hope
coming and hope fading and the
light going from their eyes

The Eternal cross is ours ours
the waiting and the sad hours of
watching and the suffering
ours

Here is the coloured flame of men
sowing and reaping and wandering
upon the earth – here are the hours
of toiling the pain and the horror
of hours relentless and hours without
Hope – here is the uncared earth
and the broken barn the scattered
hay and the rotting wood
Here is the Life of M A N and the Death
of L I F E and here the Wooden Cross
the Burning Shining Cross
high on the fading hill scattering
the myriad ashes to the rushing winds
and the high tempests carrying
the Word to the Peoples of the Earth

and the Earth's People pausing cease
from their work and gather the fallen ashes
ashes cast on the pregnant Earth
and Life springs to the changing hours
Hours proclaiming the saving of Man
Man saved Life saved and all the
Peoples of the Earth

Thy People arise and carry Thy Words
Thy Words are carried and Thy People secure
Let not the Holy Vision fade
Lest Thy People weaken
And Thy Word Be Lost
And All That Which Thou Hast Made

ROSEMARY SUTCLIFF

The Feast of Lights

This is the Feast of Lights.
  We have put the holly and the ivy up; a sprig or two
Behind each picture, three behind the largest;
As it was in my father's time, and his father's before him, world without
end.
  The scented candle, gift of a friend far off, is lit before the crib.
Spicy, aromatic, warm and faintly bitter, censing the whole house
As though three kings had just walked through it.
The flame still flutters from their passing, then steadies, casting
The upward shadow of puzzled, manger-nuzzling ox onto painted sky
of stars.

This is the Feast of Lights.
  Look behind you into the shadows.

Man wakes and rubs his eyes and looks about him, says 'I am!'
And then 'Because I am, there must be something more. If not,
I shall run mad from loneliness, shut in the solitude of my own skin.
There must be One who made me and all my kind, and the barley
Springing from the scratched furrow, and the young of the cattle herd,
And the warm days of goodness lying in the sun;
That we may be, all of us, part each of other, in the One, and not alone.'
The warm days pass and the Great Cold comes, and the Long Dark,
And the earth is turned to frightening stone that will not let the barley
through.
And man says 'God is dying! His light droops further,
Further down the sky. See, I will make a fire, a great light

To help You with its strength and power and Life;
To show You the way back.
We are together in this, You and I.
God! Don't die!'

    So in the darkness of the year man lights his fire,
And presently the Dark passes and the Cold is driven back;
And it is Spring.
    And again it happens, and again, and on and on, and the people grow
To understand. This is the pattern. God must die,
And live, and die and live again; only so
Will the barley quicken and the cattle bring forth young.
    'Except a grain of wheat fall to the ground and die . . .'
They give more now than once they gave. Not only fire but Life
Itself in the flames; Life of Man to strengthen Life of God.
Now God and Man, God and Sacrifice, are part each of the other.
It has become a deeper thing.
    And then at last, so short a time ago, as men remember time,
That it might be yesterday – or still tomorrow – God says 'Now I
Will make the Sacrifice.
And My making shall be once and for always, and complete.'

    The candle flickers before the crib,
Censing the whole house as though three kings had just passed through
    it,
Carrying gold and frankincense – and myrrh.

This is the Feast of Lights.

GEOFFREY TREASE

Satan on the Fives Court (1928)

To Satan flying casually there came a tolling bell
That called the boys to school for prayers, and made him sigh for Hell.
Their prayers were so mechanical that he was little vexed
And settled on the fives-court roof to see what happened next.
The O.T.C. came streaming out in field-day panoply,
And Satan winked his ancient eye and tapped his hooves in glee.

'Is memory dimmed so swiftly of the passion and the pain?
Are good pre-war conditions so soon restored again?
Is that dreamed hour forgotten when they heard the barrage cease
And Spring came in November with the bugles of the Peace?
Ten years ago the echo of those bugles struck the sky.
The sound is now forgotten that they thought would never die.
The War is barely finished, the war to finish war,
And see the fine old public schools preparing hard for more!'

Just then the sergeant-major, all majestic and aloof,
Appeared – and Satan's laughter nearly rolled him off the roof.
The column then moved off in fours, went swinging through the arch.
The Devil thought sardonically, 'How gallantly they march!'
The blaring music faded in the traffic of the street,
And Satan smiled and rose again upon his tireless feet.

The Middle-Aged

You old ones say we young are always tragic.
  Perhaps. But you have made the tragedy –
You, gross and dull, who can't recall the magic
  The world once held for you – the poetry,
Lost causes to be fought for . . . You, forgetting
  The mist-hung road on which you turned your backs,
Turned to your Sunday papers and your betting,
  Your smoke-room tales, cigars and income tax.

If we are discontented, is it strange?
  We know you had our dreams. Shall we too say,
'Too young to start yet,' then 'Too old to change'?
  Shall we, too, pass unsatisfied away?
Rather we strive to keep, O worldly wise,
The vision that once shone in your young eyes.

The Apple-Tree

I must be swift and plant my apple-tree
  Where the builders have left their wilderness
Of sand and broken brick – or I'll not see
  The imagined garden putting on the dress
Whose lines and tints we dreamed, and the young tree
  Spreading its silver arms in loveliness.
I must be swift. And you – be swift for me.
  Lift soon your misty blossoms to caress
The stooping clouds, before War's devilry
  Makes here a second shattered wilderness.

ARNOLD WESKER

All Things Tire of Themselves

*On the occasion of
my fiftieth birthday, 24 May 1982*

All things tire of themselves
Be glad.
Like passion
The demagogue's tongue
The revolutionary's fervour
The singer's joy
The heart's sadness.
Be glad. Be comforted.

Be comforted
That all things tire of themselves.
For with recrimination and rancour
Go longing for revenge
The tiny satisfactions of spite
Not only hope, despair also.
And passion.
All tire, tire of themselves.
Be glad. Be comforted.

Look how the sun hurries its last minutes
The ache wearies
The crying cannot go on
Though the smile fades.
Remember the loved melody overplayed
That falls apart,

New words too loud and overused
Ceasing to make sense.
But silence too
That tires of itself.
Be comforted.
All things, all things.
And passion.

Ah! how can that be, we wonder,
How can such energy and joy
Come to an end? It does.
And love. It does.
And sweet belief that chaos can be ordered
Faith people can be reasoned.
It does. It does.
All things tire of themselves
Childhood of its childishness
Youth of its certitude
Manhood of bravery.
And passion.
Passion tires of itself. Be comforted.

Be comforted.
If confidence falters
And holy grails fade
Unhappiness wearies also.
The mocking wear their shrillness thin
Contempt withers
The sneer dissolves
Bored cynics expire.
All things, all things tire of themselves.
Be comforted and glad.
All things.
The city of its dreams
Evil of its tyranny
The long storm of its turbulence
Even sweet reason.
And passion.

Ah! can passion tire of itself?
Can it ever be, we wonder
Happy with the heights
All images sharp and glowing
Language on edge
Our usage precise
Inventive, humour-bright
And all nerves ringing ringing?
But it can be.
Passion does tire of itself.
It does. It does.
As all things do.
Be glad. Be comforted.

And if madness follows
Will that not tire of itself
As all things do? Be glad.
For though no joy lasts
No pain lingers.
Nothing is sustained
But knowledge this is so.
Be glad. Be comforted.

Old Men

Old men cry out in their sleep
Dream vivid dreams of youth
They cannot keep down
The pain of passing years
Sleeping or awake catch up
With the young man who has raced on
Nor stem the dreams' tears.

Weep for them, the old men, weep
For them and theirs.
The pain of all their passing years.

Old men sit wondering at themselves
Caught by the cunning silence
Of the spider
Misled, betrayed, their heads confused, spinning
Full of time's web of remembered images.
No one had told them time goes
No one had warned.
Who knows such things
When youth is not a dream
And the girls sing and the blood sings?

Weep for them, the old men, weep
For them and theirs.
The pain, the pain of all their passing years.

To All My Children

You must not attempt honesty
It is impossible.
You will be misunderstood
Abused
By those who brought Prometheus low.

You must not trust your heart around
It embarrasses.
Besides
Who was the friend misled you
Said that you could comprehend the cunning thing?

You must not lay your cards down
Call a spade a spade.
Often it is not
Rather
It becomes the tool they twain you with.

Nobody will thank you for a truth
That is merely yours.
And who is it you think you are
Daring
To bring fire hot upon their heads?

Fierce indignant foes await you
Judges like pubs on every corner
Drunk with their narrow certitudes
A pint of answers in their hands
Intoxicated eyes ablaze with self-contempt
And fear of your sobriety.
Who is it you think you are
Trying to be honest
Confidently laying down your cards
A poker hand of spades

Your heart too good to be believed
When they and they alone
Are Jesus Christ's inebriated men and true?

From 'Three Poems for My Daughter Tanya Jo on Her Twenty-First Birthday', 25 May 1982

TWO
I would take upon me all for you
Pain me your pain
Your sadness bear
Your tears weep
Mistakes make mine
And shames keep
Deep in my old soul.
Oh that I could for you!

But I cannot, there it is!
There it is, that life
In which one day
You will be no one's daughter.

Prepare, daughter,
Prepare for what I cannot
Do and die for you
Though I would for you
For ever for you;
But there it is
I cannot for you.

I wish that only had been passed
The finest of my genes to you.
Irresolute ones lost
The foolish spent

Bewildered ones destroyed
Those of weakness
Cowardice, fear
Foolhardiness, despair
Dispersed.
But there it is, they were not.
You have all, daughter.

Everything and all
That in you rages
Hurts, intoxicates,
Concoct with what spice and pain
And spare imagination
I've endowed you
The best around you.
I cannot for you,
Though I would all, all for you.

I Marvel at These Things

I marvel at these things:
Who conceived the wheel?
Where is he remembered?
Who first gazed and gazed at the seed
Upon whom dawned, in that dawn,
Here all begins?
Who shepherded
Then twisted his intelligence
Round the sheep's back
To spin warmth from the chaotic storms?
I marvel at the unravelling of chaos.
I marvel at these things.

I marvel at these things:
Who dared pluck the first fruit,
Risked the unknown taste of things?
Took courage and fire in his hands?
Regarded rocks with fantasies
He could not know he possessed
But guessed gold was there,
Smote steel, struck coal
And greedily perceived the gem?
Which is the man, is he named
Who combed seas, understood
There was a task to be done
And he could, of all strange creatures,
He could?
I marvel at these things.

T. H. WHITE

Reading Giraldus Cambrensis

Look at the peace of inanimate things,
The sanity of stones,
The probity of pasture fields, dead trees,
Old hills and patient bones.

Giraldus tells us that the Archbishop stood
To preach at Parc-y-Cappel
'On a verdant plain' – wherefore the people
Built there a chapel.

This bishop in eleven eighty-eight
Preached them the Third Crusade.
(A footnote adds that 'Chapel Field' now marks
The sermon that he made.)

Think, when at Parc-y-Cappel, what young Taffy
Here took the Cross.
Did he sing, marching Europe, sad Welsh hymns
And look at a loss?

Think of that stream of miserable men,
The half not knowing
Where, with their mormals, rags and wretched staffs,
They were meekly going.

Think of the Sickness of the Hoste, the famine,
The ant-like army's woe,

Betrayed by leaders, knackered by black Arabs,
Eight hundred years ago.

The sorrow-serpent wound by that Archbishop
Has wound away its pain:
But Chapel Field, now churchless, is once more
A verdant plain.

Look at the peace of inanimate things,
The sanity of stones,
The probity of pasture fields, dead trees,
Old hills and patient bones.

Journey's End

I've been a bitter friend to you,
And you to me.
It was a bitter hour that bore us two,
And a black day, my dearest love, that brought us through
So many miles of land and sea;
Through more than twenty years of different days,
Through time and space,
Through severance to be
Never more severed.
Oh, you'll not forget me. Our two ways
May break apart and stormily retrace
The miles of land and sea and years and time and space
That our two lines unconsciously endeavoured
Towards meeting, back from meeting.
But, my hard heart, my bitter sweeting,
This was no moon affair; we have shed no tears,
And no, you'll not forget me;
Not in forty years.

On Falling in Love Again after Seven Years

These living bodies that we wear
So change by every seventh year
That in a new dress we appear.

Andrew Young

In seven years this aching nude
Has all its particles renewed.
Each organ, sinew, bit of bone,
Now turned to stone, now turned to stone,
Will grow again and from within
Refill a new, forgetful skin.
The ache will go, the woe be done,
In time to meet another one.

Medusa One, Medusa Two,
Well, I have done with both of you,
And must, with seven years' slow pain,
Re-grow the tissues once again.
The heart, now stony-broke, will mend
And seek in time a final friend,
And she, who shall be all to me,
Shall be addressed: Medusa Three.

But when Medusa Three departs
What way can men re-grow their hearts?
Unresilient, defeated,
Hopeless and puzzled, old and cheated,
No seven years left in which to slough
The skin and make another Now?
Then will come Medusa Four.
Into her Grave my heart will pour.

The Tower of Siloam

[Luke xiii, 4]

Is it correct to sing in rhyme
Tragedy's boredom? Is it right to tell
The fatuous common side of time,
The innocent dead without crime
On whom the Tower of Siloam fell?

A million mothers weep today
Sons lost by nothing more than growth.
A million sweethearts sigh to say
'It did not happen in that way:
It fell for one – not neither – nor for both.'

There – at that Tick – with clash and shock
The twelve-year-old, his father's tender care,
Slid under the bus. And his clock
Went, between Tick and hoped-for Tock,
Mixed with a bicycle, no one knows where.

And is it wise or kind to add
To aching Sweetheart or to Dad,
They will forget; they won't be sad?
Sons do go, and it matters not a jot
Whether the Tower of Siloam fell or not.

Letter from a Goose-Shooter

On Inniskea, long before Patrick came,
Stood the stone idol of the secret name:
The magic people made him. No surprise,
No threat, no question lit his two round eyes,
Nor had he other features. Consciousness
Was all his feeling, all his creed 'I wis.'
He watched the wild geese twenty centuries.

Inniskea is an island. Ten years gone
The human race lived here, the windows shone
With candles over the water, and men
Fished currachs, women wellwards went from ben.
There was a King to rule the island then,
Chosen for might, who had his Admiral
Of All the Inniskeas. The priest's sick call
Was this cold pasture's only festival.

Mass was so far off, with such storms between,
And in the dark nights moved so much unseen
On the wild waters, that Man's beating heart
Still sometimes turned towards the old God's art.
Much magic was made with the dew. The wells
Secretly stirred with strange internal spells.

To keep the Agent off, or the Excise,
Fires were lit before the God of Eyes
And dances made around his stone, sunwise.
Their old cold Godstone they, for comfort, dressed
In one new suit each year: his Sunday best.

Then the remorseless sea, the all-beleaguering,
The crafty, long-combed sea, the stark and whistling,
The savage, ancient sea, master at waiting,
Struck once.
   Two hours later the Mainland
Received one man, a saucepan in his hand,
Astride an upturned currach. At the Inn

They gave him clothes without, whisky within,
Such as they could: but he nor left nor right
Altered his eyes. Only with all his might,
This man bailed with his saucepan all that night.
In half one hour of squall, from calm to calm, the Main
Holding his ten mates drowned had fallen on asleep again.

Nobody painted the houses after.
The islanders lost all heart for laughter.
Work was a weariness, dances were done,
On the island whose pride of Man was gone.

Now I am all alone on Inniskea,
All alone with the wind and with the sea.
The corrugated iron, rusted brown,
Gives a burnt look to the abandoned town.
The roofs are ruins and the walls are down.

The Land Commission took the people ashore.
King Phillip Lavell is here no more.
They have even taken away the God Who Saw,
To stand in Dublin Museum. From ten till four
He eyes the opposite wall.
               Oh, God of Eyes,
Bound there in darkness and deprived of skies,
Know that your Geese are back. Know that their cries
Lag on the loud wind as, by candlelight,
At Inniskea's one fire I, your last subject, write:
Lulled by their laughter, cradled in their night.

ANGUS WILSON

Cri de Cœur

An English Professor at Yale
Was found looking sickly and pale.
   The novel he'd structured
   Had suddenly ruptured,
And nothing was left of the tale.

A. N. WILSON

Hospital Visit

We could not fight there, even if she chose.
Someone had strapped a drip on to her arm,
And stuck some plastic tubing up her nose.
It was no time for gossip, lies or charm.
I kissed her cheek, and watched her eyelids tremble:
A reconciliation, of a sort.
It spared the need to flatter or dissemble,
There would be other times. Then I'd explain,
   I thought.
At least, maddeningly, she was there.
I'd come again.

   And was she then aware,
How soon embarrassing, unspoken fears
Would be fulfilled? For I was not.
I did not even get the chance to say
How sad the year of our estrangement got.

She would have laughed to bursting at the way
I could not see her funeral for tears.

Ballade of the Bishop and the Empty Tomb

The Bishop of Durham has ... given the impression (quite wrongly) that he does
not believe in the Resurrection, whereas his doubts concern the Empty Tomb.

Norman St John Stevas, *The Times*, 27 September 1984

When English bishops chant the ancient creed,
'Born of the Virgin Mary' they must say,
But from the See of Durham it's decreed
We needn't take this in a literal way.
Born, well, perhaps; of Mary, yes, indeed.
But as for being born of virgin womb,
They're sceptical, just as they'd all concede
Their honest doubts about the Empty Tomb.

The early witnesses, we're all agreed,
Were the products of the thinking of their day.
They might have seen him suffer, die and bleed,
But had they a Theology M.A.
The Easter message might have changed indeed.
And from the Garden to the Upper Room
They might have run with quaking voice to breed
Their honest doubts about the Empty Tomb.

Do not mistake our bishops; they will lead
The flock from prejudice about the way
In which the slaves of sin, of death, were freed
Upon the first ambiguous Easter Day.
They'll never let us quite forget the need
For tolerance and balance: though there's room
For words like *Resurrection*, don't impede
Their honest doubts about the Empty Tomb.

Envoi

Prince Jesus, heal the blindness of our eyes,
That after death, through Purgatory's gloom,
We all may see the Glory that did rise
And left behind, on Earth, an Empty Tomb.

P. G. WODEHOUSE

The Visitors

[In July 1955, Nancy Spain, chief literary critic of the Beaverbrook press, in
company with Lord Noel-Buxton, attempted to make an unannounced call upon
Evelyn Waugh at his home. Waugh ejected the pair with characteristic acerbity.
Subsequently, both Nancy Spain and Waugh wrote amusing accounts of the
incident, which attracted a good deal of publicity.]

My dear old dad, when I was a lad
    Planning my life's career,
Said 'Read for the bar, be a movie star
Or travel around in lands afar
    As a mining engineer,
But don't, whatever you do,' he hissed,
'Be a popular, widely-read novelist,'
    And he went on to explain
That if you're an author, sure as fate,
Maybe early or maybe late,
Two hearty pests will come crashing the gate,
    Noel-Buxton and Nancy Spain.

    Noel-Buxton and Nancy Spain, my lad,
        Noel-Buxton and Nancy Spain.
    They're worse, he said, than a cold in the head
        Or lunch on an English train.
    Some homes have beetles and some have mice,
    Neither of which are very nice,
    But an author's home has (he said this twice)
        Noel-Buxton and Nancy Spain.

Well, I said 'Indeed?', but I paid no heed
   To the warning words I quote:
For I hoped, if poss., to make lots of dross
And to be the choice of the old Book Soc.,
   So I wrote and wrote and wrote.
Each novel I published hit the spot:
There wasn't a dud in all the lot.
   And things looked right as rain,
When as one day at my desk I sat,
The front door knocker went rat-tat-tat,
And who was it waiting on the mat?
   Noel-Buxton and Nancy Spain.

Now, all you young men who hope with your pen
   To climb to the top of the tree,
Just pause and think ere you dip in the ink
That you may be standing upon the brink
   Of the thing that happened to me.
That strong, stark book you are writing now
May be good for a sale of fifty thou',
   But it's wisest to refrain:
For what will it boot though it brings to you
   A yacht and a car and a page in *Who's Who*,
If you also get, as you're sure to do,
   Noel-Buxton and Nancy Spain?

   Noel-Buxton and Nancy Spain, my lads,
      Noel-Buxton and Nancy Spain.
   Just see, I implore, that you keep on the door
      A short and sturdy chain.
   Slugs are unpleasant and so are fleas,
   And I wouldn't much care to be stung by bees,
   But far, far better are those than these,
      Noel-Buxton and Nancy Spain.

Printer's Error

As o'er my latest book I pored,
    Enjoying it immensely,
I suddenly exclaimed 'Good Lord!'
    And gripped the volume tensely.
'Golly!' I cried. I writhed in pain.
'They've done it on me once again!'
    And furrows creased my brow.
I'd written (which I thought quite good)
'Ruth, ripening into womanhood,
Was now a girl who knocked men flat
And frequently got whistled at.'
And some vile, careless, casual gook
Had spoiled the best thing in the book
    By printing 'not'
    (Yes, 'not', great Scott!)
        When I had written 'now'.

On murder in the first degree
    The Law, I knew, is rigid:
Its attitude, if A kills B,
    To A is always frigid.
It counts it not a trivial slip
If on behalf of authorship
You liquidate compositors.
This kind of conduct it abhors
    And seldom will allow.
Nevertheless, I deemed it best
And in the public interest
To buy a gun, to oil it well,
Inserting what is called a shell,
    And go and pot
    With sudden shot
    This printer who had printed 'not'
        When I had written 'now'.

I tracked the bounder to his den
    Through private information:
I said, 'Good afternoon,' and then
    Explained the situation:
'I'm not a fussy man,' I said.
'I smile when you put "rid" for "red"
And "bad" for "bed" and "hoad" for "head"
    And "bolge" instead of "bough".
When "wone" appears in lieu of "wine"
Or if you alter "Cohn" to "Schine",*
    I never make a row.
I know how easy errors are.
But this time you have gone too far
By printing "not" when you knew what
    I really wrote was "now".
    Prepare,' I said, 'to meet your God
    Or, as you'd say, your Goo or Bod
        Or possibly your Gow.'

A few weeks later into court
    I came to stand my trial.
The Judge was quite a decent sort,
    He said, 'Well, cocky, I'll
Be passing sentence in a jiff,
And so, my poor unhappy stiff,
If you have anything to say,
Now is the moment. Fire away.
    You have?'
    I said, 'And how!
Me lud, the facts I don't dispute.
I did, I own it freely, shoot
This printer through the collar stud.

* Mr Cohn and Mr Schine, two youthful agents of 'Black Joe' McCarthy and his
'Un-American Activities Committee', attracted a good deal of ridicule when they visited
England as 'anti-Communist investigators' in the early nineteen-fifties.

What else could I have done, me lud?
   He'd printed "not" ...'
   The Judge said, '*What!*
      When you had written "now"?
God bless my soul! Gadzooks!' said he.
'The blighters once did that to me.
   A dirty trick, I trow.
I hereby quash and override
The jury's verdict. Gosh!' he cried.
'Give me your hand. Yes, I insist,
You splendid fellow! Case dismissed.'
   (Cheers, and a Voice, 'Wow-wow!')

A statue stands against the sky,
   Lifelike and rather pretty.
'Twas recently erected by
   The PEN committee.
And many a passer-by is stirred.
For on the plinth, if that's the word,
In golden letters you may read
'This is the man who did the deed.
   His hand set to the plough,
He did not sheathe the sword, but got
A gun at great expense and shot
The human blot who'd printed "not"
   When he had written "now".
He acted with no thought of self,
Not for advancement, not for pelf,
But just because it made him hot
To think the man had printed "not"
   When he had written "now".'

AUTHORS' BIOGRAPHIES

Richard Adams
Born 1920. Bradfield and Worcester College, Oxford. Five and a half wartime years in the army, twenty-five years in the Civil Service. Five novels, plus a few other books. Married, two daughters. F.R.S.L.

Alan Ayckbourn
Haileybury. Playwright and theatre director. One ex-wife. Two sons. One cat. No previously published poems.

Beryl Bainbridge
Born Liverpool, 1934. Eleven novels, several plays. Overworked, and grateful.

Rachel Billington
Novelist, playwright and critic. Nine adult novels, including *A Woman's Age* and, 1985, *The Garish Day*. Two children's novels including, 1984, *Star-Time*. Two TV plays, four radio plays. Married, with four children.

Ronald Blythe
Born in Suffolk and has lived all his writing life in East Anglia. Has published poems, short stories, a novel, essays, criticism and history. He describes his latest book, *Divine Landscapes*, as 'a kind of sacred geography'.

Malcolm Bradbury
Born 1932. Professor of American Studies, University of East Anglia. Critic, television playwright and novelist. Four novels, including *The History Man* and *Rates of Exchange*. Married, with two sons.

John Braine
Born 1922 in Bradford, Yorkshire. A librarian from 1940 to 1957, with intervals in the Royal Navy, starving in a bedsitter in Kensington, and in hospital. His first novel, *Room at the Top*, released him from librarianship in 1957. Before it's too late, would like to be a poet again. Lives now in Hampstead, very happily.

Neville Braybrooke
Born 1925. Began his literary career when he was sixteen, as the editor of *The Wind and the Rain* (1941–51). His poems have appeared in the *New Statesman* and the *Tablet*, and been broadcast and televised by the B.B.C.

Raymond Briggs
Born 1934. Wimbledon School of Art and Slade School. Book illustrator and designer, writer and cartoonist. More recently, has been designing for the stage and has written two stage plays and a radio play.

Brigid Brophy
Born 1929. Oxford (classics). Novelist and critic. Married (to novelist and Director of National Gallery): daughter, grandson. Vegan; arguer for Animal Rights. Co-organizer of successful campaign for Public Lending Rights. Crippled since 1984 by multiple sclerosis.

J. M. Coetzee
Born 1940. Lives in South Africa. Novelist and academic.

Quentin Crisp
Born on Christmas Day, 1908, in England, but has now seen the light and lives in America. Educated (if at all) at Denstone College in Derbyshire. Writes books (chiefly about himself) including *How to Have a Life Style*, *The Naked Civil Servant*, *How to Become a Virgin* and *Manners from Heaven*, and articles for magazines (chiefly about the movies).

Roald Dahl
Born Llandaff, South Wales, 1916. Has published four volumes of short stories, one novel and fifteen children's books which include *Charlie and the Chocolate Factory*, *James and the Giant Peach* and *The B.F.G.* Married, four children.

Sally Emerson
Author of two novels, *Second Sight* (which won a *Yorkshire Post* prize for the best first work of the year) and *Listeners*. An editor of *Books and Bookmen*. Married, one daughter.

John Fowles
Born 1926. Novelist and part-time museum curator.

Antonia Fraser
Born 1932. The Dragon School (a boys' preparatory school), a Catholic convent
and Oxford. Author of three historical biographies and *The Weaker Vessel:
Women in 17th Century England*. Also five mysteries featuring Jemima Shore,
Investigator. Has edited several anthologies, including *Scottish Love Poems* and
Oxford and Oxfordshire In Verse.

Athol Fugard
Born 1932. Playwright. Bird-watching and wild flowers.

Alan Garner
Born 1934. Manchester Grammar School and Oxford. Nine novels and five
children.

Stella Gibbons
Born 1902. North London Collegiate School and University College, London.
Poet and novelist. Three books of verse, twenty-seven novels, three books of
short stories. Married, one daughter.

Victoria Glendinning
Prizewinning biographer of Elizabeth Bowen, Edith Sitwell, Vita Sackville-
West. Literary journalist, principally for the *Sunday Times*. Twice married. Four
sons.

Rumer Godden
Born 1907. Brought up mostly in India. Educated privately. Novelist. Writer of
children's books, film scripts. Married.

William Golding
Born 1911. Marlborough Grammar School, Brasenose College, Oxford. Novelist
and essayist. Nobel Laureate, 1983.

L. P. Hartley
1895–1972. Harrow and Balliol. Service in Great War 1916–18. First book
published 1924. James Tait Black Memorial Prize, 1947, for *Eustace and Hilda*, the
third volume of the trilogy so named. W. H. Heinemann Foundation Prize for
The Go-Between, 1953. Several other novels. Clark Lecturer, Cambridge, 1964.
Companion of Literature, 1972.

William Horwood
Born 1944. Bristol University. *Daily Mail* journalist, then full-time author. One
non-fiction, three novels.

Francis King
Born Switzerland, 1923. Childhood in India. Shrewsbury and Balliol College, Oxford. Fifteen years in British Council. First published works poetry. Novelist, drama-critic (*Sunday Telegraph*), novel-reviewer (*Spectator*).

R. M. Lamming
Born 1949. From the Isle of Man. Educated at boarding school in Wales and Oxford. Novels and short stories. She won the 1983 David Higham Prize for Fiction.

Doris Lessing
Born 1919 in Persia. Lived in Southern Rhodesia, and then London. Author of *The Golden Notebook, Briefing for a Descent into Hell, The Memoirs of a Survivor, The Grass is Singing, The Summer Before the Dark, The Diaries of Jane Somers, The Good Terrorist* (published autumn 1985), the novel sequences 'The Children of Violence' and 'Canopus in Argos', and several volumes of short stories. Also a slim volume called *Fourteen Poems*.

C. S. Lewis
1898–1963. Malvern and Oxford. A book of poems published in 1919 and another in 1926 while a don at Oxford. Two collections have been published posthumously. Also published works of literary criticism, science fiction, children's novels and Christian apologetics. Professor at Cambridge, 1955–63.

David Lodge
Born 1935. Novelist, critic and, at present, Professor of Modern English Literature at the University of Birmingham. Author of seven novels and several works of literary criticism.

Olivia Manning
1908–1980. Portsmouth Girls' School. Novelist. Worked for Medici and in various news organizations in the Balkans, Cairo, Jerusalem, etc. Author of a travel book about Ireland, a biography of H. M. Stanley and *Extraordinary Cats*.

Arthur Marshall
Born 1910. Oundle and Cambridge. Broadcaster, writer, columnist, script-reader and TV performer.

Naomi Mitchison
Born 1897. Written about eighty books, from solid history to fairy tales. Five children, nineteen grandchildren, five great-grandchildren.

John Moore
1907–67. Born Tewkesbury, Gloucestershire. Educated Malvern. Author of several books on country matters, including the Brensham trilogy, *Portrait of Elmbury, Brensham Village* and *The Blue Field*; also *The White Sparrow, Dance and Skylark, The Season of the Year, Come Rain Come Shine*, etc. F.R.S.L.

Jan Morris
Born 1926. Used to be James Morris. Has written many books about places, three about the British Empire and one about herself.

Iris Murdoch
Born 1919 in Dublin. Badminton and Oxford. Philosopher and novelist.

Enoch Powell
Born 1912. King Edward's, Birmingham and Trinity, Cambridge. Royal Warwickshire Regiment, 1939–46. An M.P. since 1950.

Jean Rhys
1890–1979. Born Dominica, West Indies. Author of the following novels: *Quartet* (1928), *After Leaving Mr Mackenzie* (1930), *Voyage in the Dark* (1934), *Good Morning Midnight* (1939), *Wide Sargasso Sea* (1966).

Paul Scott
1920–1978. His first novel was *Johnny Sahib*. The television series 'Jewel in the Crown' was based on his 'Raj Quartet'. His last novel, *Staying On*, won the Booker Prize in 1977.

Rosemary Sutcliff
Born 1920. Privately educated in North Devon. Now lives in Sussex. Two dogs. Approximately forty-five books to date.

Geoffrey Trease
Born 1909. Nottingham High School and Oxford. Wrote much verse in youth before becoming full-time author in 1933, producing since then over ninety works – novels, history, biography, autobiography, criticism and children's books, as well as plays, radio and television drama. F.R.S.L. and past chairman of the Society of Authors.

Arnold Wesker
Born 1932, London. Playwright, director, three books of short stories, two of essays, one for young people. Married, three children plus. Hopes to write a lot of poetry at around sixty. Contemplating learning to draw and paint.

T. H. White
1906–64. Cambridge. Taught for several years in 1930s before devoting himself to writing. Best known for his four books on the Arthurian legends, 'The Once and Future King', completed in 1958.

Angus Wilson
Born 1913. Novelist and critic; has written biographies of Zola, Dickens and Kipling.

A. N. Wilson
Born 1950. Novelist, biographer and literary journalist. His latest novel is *Gentlemen in England*.

P. G. Wodehouse
1881–1975. Dulwich College. Novelist, short-story writer, playwright and poet. Creator of such famous characters as Jeeves and Bertie Wooster. Became U.S. citizen in 1955.

PUBLISHER'S ACKNOWLEDGEMENTS

The publisher is grateful to the following authors and copyright holders for permission to reproduce the poems contained in this anthology:

RICHARD ADAMS, 'The Green Flash', 'The Albatross', 'Red Hair', 'Insomnia' and 'Iris Murdoch', copyright © Richard Adams, 1986.

ALAN AYCKBOURN, 'Seven Fragments', copyright © Haydonning Ltd, 1986. By permission of the author and Haydonning Ltd.

BERYL BAINBRIDGE, 'Three Poems' and 'Vatican Trouble', copyright © Beryl Bainbridge, 1986. By permission of the author.

RACHEL BILLINGTON, 'Catherine' and 'Peace', copyright © Rachel Billington, 1986. By permission of the author and David Higham Associates Ltd.

RONALD BLYTHE, 'Charles Edward' and 'Sligo, September 17th, 1948', copyright © Ronald Blythe, 1986. By permission of the author.

MALCOLM BRADBURY, 'An Uninvited Guest', 'Evening Class', 'The Pilgrim Fathers in Bloomington, Indiana' and 'Wanting Names for Things' (first published in *Two Poets* by Allan Rodway and Malcolm Bradbury, The Byron Press, Nottingham, 1966), copyright © Malcolm Bradbury, 1966. By permission of the author and The Byron Press.

JOHN BRAINE, 'Your Word is Moorland' and 'Slacken the Pace of Prison' (first published in *An Anthology of Contemporary Northern Poetry*, Harrap, 1947), copyright © John Braine, 1947. By permission of the author.

NEVILLE BRAYBROOKE, 'Joseph Speaks' (first published in the *Tablet*, 18 December 1976), copyright © Neville Braybrooke, 1976; 'Sheep' (*Tablet*, 5 January 1980), copyright © Neville Braybrooke, 1980; 'The Wise Men' (*Tablet*, 19 June 1981), copyright © Neville Braybrooke, 1981; 'An Old Actor' (first published in *New Poems* 8, ed. John Fuller, Hutchinson, 1982), copyright © Neville Braybrooke, 1982. By permission of the author.

RAYMOND BRIGGS, 'Jean, 1975', copyright © Raymond Briggs, 1986. By permission of the author.

BRIGID BROPHY, 'Nocturne', 'Snow, 1980' and 'Concourse', copyright © Brigid Brophy, 1986. By permission of the author.

J. M. COETZEE, 'Dusk Seeps up the Entrail ...' (first published in *Staffrider*, Ravan Press, Braamfontein, South Africa, March 1978), copyright © J. M. Coetzee, 1978. By permission of the author.

QUENTIN CRISP, 'Now I am Dead', copyright © Quentin Crisp, 1986. By permission of the author.

'Acknowledgements', copyright © R. M. Lamming, 1986. By permission of the author.

DORIS LESSING, 'Here' (first published in the *New Statesman*, 17 June 1966), copyright © Doris Lessing, 1966; 'A Visit' (*New Statesman*, 4 November 1966), copyright © Doris Lessing, 1966; 'The Islands' (*Listener*, December 1967), copyright © Doris Lessing, 1967; 'A Small Girl Throws Stones at a Swan in Regents Park' and 'Hunger the King' (*New Statesman*, 24 November 1967), copyright © Doris Lessing, 1967. By permission of the author and Jonathan Clowes Ltd.

C. S. LEWIS, 'Hermione in the House of Paulina' (first published in *Augury: An Oxford Miscellany of Verse and Prose*, ed. Alec M. Hardie and Keith C. Douglas, Basil Blackwell, 1940; revised version published in *Poems*, ed. Walter Hooper, Collins/Geoffrey Bles, 1964), copyright © C. S. Lewis Pte Ltd, 1940, 1964. By permission of William Collins Plc. 'Leaving for Ever the Home of One's Youth' and 'Finchley Avenue', copyright © C. S. Lewis Pte Ltd, 1986. By permission of Curtis Brown Ltd.

DAVID LODGE, 'Epitaph for a Film Star' (first published in the *Spectator*, 19 October 1962), copyright © David Lodge, 1962; 'A Martian Goes to College' (*London Review of Books*, November 1984), copyright © David Lodge, 1984; 'Snow in Suburbia', copyright © David Lodge, 1986. By permission of the author.

OLIVIA MANNING, 'Written in the Third Year of the War' and 'Black Cat', copyright © the Estate of Olivia Manning, 1986. By permission of David Higham Associates Ltd.

ARTHUR MARSHALL, 'John Betjeman Celebrates the De-rationing of Sweets in 1954' (first published in *New Statesman Competitions*, ed. Arthur Marshall, Turnstile Press, 1955), copyright © Arthur Marshall, 1955. By permission of the author.

NAOMI MITCHISON, 'Oldies' (first published in the *New Statesman*, 4 November 1983), copyright © Naomi Mitchison, 1983; 'Mauritian Landscape', 'Lyke-Wake' and 'Midsummer 1956', copyright © Naomi Mitchison, 1986. By permission of the author.

JOHN MOORE, 'Draw Close the Curtains' (first published in *Come Rain, Come Shine*, Collins, 1956), copyright © John Moore, 1956. By permission of A. D. Peters & Co. Ltd.

JAN MORRIS, 'Pig Rhyme' (first published in *She* Magazine, December 1984), copyright © Jan Morris, 1984; 'Four Cat Couplets', copyright © Jan Morris, 1986. By permission of the author.

IRIS MURDOCH, 'Agamemnon Class 1939' (first published in the *Boston Univer-*

21/6/90
17/7/90.